"Allow me to warn you that if you have any thought of deceiving me you will regret it."

"Let me go!" She slapped his hand away from her face. "How dare you touch me!"

He smiled then, but his eyes were cold, and suddenly Georgiana was afraid.

"You presume too much up on my goodwill, Miss Westleigh. I might have seduced you at any time since our first meeting. Do you think I am made of stone?"

Hot color flooded her cheeks. "You would not," she cried wildly.

"Why not? Your character leaves much to be desired, but your face and figure do not. A man might enjoy those attributes, at least."

"You are disgusting!"

"But you are not." Swiftly he bent his head and claimed her lips. As his mouth caressed hers, Georgiana felt a curious sensation in the pit of her stomach, and the urge to draw him even closer....

Kelly

Meg Alexander

The Sweet Cheat

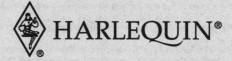

HARLEQUIN®

TORONTO • NEW YORK • LONDON
AMSTERDAM • PARIS • SYDNEY • HAMBURG
STOCKHOLM • ATHENS • TOKYO • MILAN • MADRID
PRAGUE • WARSAW • BUDAPEST • AUCKLAND

ISBN 0-373-30473-0

THE SWEET CHEAT

First North American Publication 2005

www.eHarlequin.com

Printed in U.S.A.

MEG ALEXANDER

After living in southern Spain for many years, Meg Alexander now lives in Kent, although, having been born in Lancashire, she feels that her roots are in the north of England. Meg's career has encompassed a wide variety of roles, from professional cook to assistant director of a conference center. She has always been a voracious reader, and loves to write. Other loves include history, cats, gardening, cooking and travel.

Chapter One

'Georgie, you can't mean it! You must come with me. How can I leave you here alone?' Harry Westleigh gazed at his sister in dismay.

'There is no time to argue, Hal. Lothmore's chaise will be here at any minute. Now sit on this trunk whilst I finish packing for you.' With flying fingers Georgiana continued her task. 'You have money enough for the journey?'

'Yes!' Harry's voice was muffled as he hid his face in his hands. 'But I won't abandon you to face…to face…'

'Your creditors? It won't be pleasant, I'll grant you, but better that than visit you in a debtors' prison. Here, you had best take this.' She handed him a small leather bag chinking with coins.

'You'll not gamble it away before you reach Dover?'

Her bother raised an anguished face. 'It will leave you penniless. I can't... I won't... Oh, my dear, I am so sorry...'

'It's too late for regrets!' His sister's voice was tart, but a glance at Harry's averted profile caused her to continue in a kinder tone. 'I'll join you in France, Hal, but now the important thing is for you to get away.' She glanced through the window. 'Make haste! The chaise is just turning into the street. Quickly now! We cannot know when the first of the duns will be at the door.'

Harry cast a last look around the room.

'I shan't ever see this place again,' he mourned. 'If only there were more time. Had Swarby not made up his mind to ruin me at the club last night... He called me a swindler, you know.'

'Do come along!' Georgiana caught at his sleeve, tugging him towards the doorway in her impatience. 'I'll come to Dessein's in Calais. Send me your direction as soon as you can.'

'I'll stay at Dessein's too.'

'You most certainly will not. Only think...if you are followed it is the obvious place to find you.' She pushed him ahead of her towards the staircase, following until they reached the outer door to the street.

'Wait! Let me go first. There may be someone watching even now.' With anxious eyes she peered out into the darkness, but the only sound was that of the horses snorting and stamping on the cobblestones as the chaise drew to a halt.

'All's well!' she whispered. 'Now hurry! You'll find our own coach waiting across the river!' Standing on tiptoe, she kissed his cheek, and closed the door upon his protestations. Then she sped upstairs and hurried over to the window. Long after the coach had disappeared she strained to see into the darkness, dreading the sound of pursuit, but all was silence.

At last, weak with relief, she sagged into a chair. The nervous energy which had sustained her for the past few hours had disappeared, leaving her feeling tired to death. Dully, she looked about her at a scene of chaos. Drawers lay on the floor, their contents spilling out; the bed was littered with shirts of the finest lawn, embroidered waistcoats, snowy linen stocks, handkerchiefs, and pale buckskins.

She lifted a hand to ring the bell. Then she remembered. She had dismissed the servants that very day.

She forced herself to rise to her feet. What she needed most of all was sleep. She hadn't closed her eyes the previous night, and now she felt that any further action was beyond her. It was an effort to cross the landing to her own room, and a greater one to struggle out of her gown unaided and slip into her bedrobe.

She splashed cold water on to her hands and face, dried them, and then picked up her hairbrush. As she did so she caught sight of her face in the mirror. It didn't seem possible that she could look so unchanged when her whole world had collapsed about her in less than twenty-four hours.

True, she looked tired, the milky whiteness of her skin accentuated by her fashionable crop of burnished copper curls. Against her pallor, huge green eyes glittered like an emerald sea darkened by cloud. Sick with exhaustion, she was close to tears as she threw down the brush and turned towards her bed.

Then she froze at the sound of thunderous knocking. The noise must surely rouse the neighbourhood, and she had no doubt of the likely profession of her late-night visitor. It would most certainly be a dun. Could she pretend that the house was empty? It wasn't possible. Her candles were still alight and would be visible through the chink in the curtains.

Terror banished weariness as she retraced her steps to the front door. Somehow she must throw the man off Harry's trail. She caught up a worn blue cloak hanging in the hall. One of the maids must have forgotten it. Having drawn the hood over her hair, she opened the door the merest fraction.

The thrust of a powerful shoulder sent it crashing wide before she could protest, and she jumped. The man before her was a sinister figure. Immensely tall, he filled the doorway, his bulk accentuated by a riding cloak with many capes. She could not see his face, as the lower part was hidden by his high collar, whilst the brim of his hat served to conceal his eyes.

Georgiana's mind was racing. Even in the darkness she could see that this was no dun, but it did not matter. He was still her enemy, and Harry's too. Who else would call at such an hour? Harry had canvassed all his friends for help the previous day, without success. It seemed unlikely that her visitor had come to offer succour. She must convince him that she knew nothing.

'Can I help you, sir?' She bobbed a curtsy.

'I'm here to see your master, girl.'

Without further ceremony the man pushed past her into the hall. His bearing and the authoritative tone proclaimed him every inch the aristocrat, and she stepped back in dismay. Her own gentle breeding might have been of some service in handling a dun, but this was a different matter. The man was clearly in a thundering rage. All she could do was to play the part of the ignorant servant he imagined her to be.

'Mr Westleigh is not yet returned, sir,' Georgiana bobbed another curtsy. 'Most likely you will find him at his club.'

A short, unpleasant laugh greeted this remark.

'He is not at his club, not any other, I assure you. I propose to wait for him.' The man shouldered past her without a by-your-leave, and slammed the door behind him.

'You may bring me some wine,' he said shortly. 'I'll be in here.' He threw open the nearest door and walked into the salon. 'You had best light the candles.'

Georgiana picked up a flint, but she could not control her shaking fingers as she tried to strike it.

'Here, let me! There's no need to take fright. I mean you no harm.' As he busied himself with the candles Georgiana slipped out of the room.

This was a pretty pass indeed. She could not hope to fool him for long, and she could guess his errand. He must be one of those members of the nobility whom Harry was said to have swindled. Hastily she grabbed a bottle of wine and a glass and placed them on a silver tray. With any luck he might drink deep and perhaps lost interest in an all-night vigil.

When she returned to the salon the man was lounging in a chair beside the dying embers of the fire, long legs stretched out in front of him as he tapped impatiently on a small drum-table. He eyed her without interest.

'Do you always perform your duties in that strange attire?' he questioned.

Georgiana started. She had forgotten the old cloak and the fact that the hood was drawn about her head.

'Beg pardon, sir! I was in my bed when you arrived.'

'You may retire.' He waved a dismissive hand. 'Your master's man shall attend me.'

Panic seized Georgiana. She had no wish to explain that she was alone in the house. In silence she set down the tray, turning away from him. She was unprepared for the shock when a lean brown hand shot out and gripped her by the wrist.

'Sir, please let me go,' she whined. 'I'm only a poor serving wench.'

'Are you indeed? With hands like those? Come, my dear, you can do better than that.' In a single movement he was on his feet, thrusting back the hood of her cloak. A quick tug at the strings caused the garment to fall to the ground, and Georgiana stood before him in her bedrobe.

'Wages must have increased since I was last in England,' he observed smoothly as he fingered the filmy lawn. 'This creation, if I am not much mistaken, is the work of a fashionable modiste, and has cost a fair number of golden guineas.'

He was rewarded with a glance of pure hatred from Georgiana's jade-green eyes as she looked up at him for the first time. Scarlet with confusion, she was not reassured by what she saw.

Her tormentor was a man in his middle thirties, at a guess, and there was something deeply unnerving in the mocking curve of that wide and mobile mouth. He was heavily tanned, and the blue gaze which transfixed her spoke of arrogance, authority, and a total lack of pity. He was not a man of whom she would care to beg for mercy.

She had no intention of doing so. Still rosy with embarrassment, she bent to pick up the cloak.

'Blushing? Great heavens! Is that a part of your stock-in-trade? You do well to cultivate it. It is a lost art among the ladies of the town. I must compliment Westleigh. Whatever his faults, he has taste in women.'

A careless glance swept her from head to toe. 'The figure is voluptuous, and this charming garment does little to conceal it, especially when outlined against the light.' He smiled again as he reached out to finger the neckline of her bedrobe.

Georgiana jumped as if she had been stung. It was true. Seen against the candlelight this garment left little to the imagination. With what dignity she could command she wrapped her cloak about her.

Her tormentor laughed.

'A waste of time, my dear. You cannot conceal the hair. Ah, yes, the hair...'

To Georgiana's utter fury he wound a flame-coloured strand around his fingers. 'Quite exceptional...if a little *outré*. Is the colour your own, my dear?'

Georgiana raised a hand to strike him, but he was too quick for her. Her wrist was held so fast that she gasped with pain.

'I should not consider it,' he advised. 'Now tell me, where is your paramour?'

Dropping all pretence, Georgiana faced him squarely.

'My *brother,*' she emphasised heavily, 'is well beyond your reach. You may say what you have to say to me.'

The stranger stared at her. 'He cannot have left you to face the music? I suppose it is only to be expected...'

'How dare you speak of him so? You know nothing...of the circumstances.'

'I fear I do. I have a younger brother myself. I was not overly pleased, to put it mildly, to return from the West Indies to find him in deep financial trouble, caused, I believe, by Westleigh.'

'They are not the first to make unwise investments.' Georgiana flew at once to her brother's defence. 'Cleverer men than they have come to grief...'

'Through fraud?'

'No, no! That cannot be! Harry would not...could not...'

'How else would you describe a promise to provide annuities in return for a cash lump sum, and then be unable to honour the commitment?'

'But he will... He must...'

'My dear young lady, he cannot. The money is

gone, I suspect, on supporting a lifestyle which neither he nor my brother can afford. It involved gambling, horses, and, if you'll forgive me for mentioning such indelicate matters, the support of certain ladies of the town.'

'I do not believe you,' Georgiana said, wavering. 'Harry could not have planned such a scheme. He is not clever enough.'

The words brought a look of contempt to her companion's face.

'He was clever enough to take the money and use it,' came the biting reply. 'now he must face the consequences.'

Georgiana paled to the lips, swaying where she stood.

'Nay, you shall not pretend that you did not know.' The man put out a hand to steady her, but she pulled away as if his touch would burn her. 'Look about you, Miss Westleigh. You have lived to the hilt, it would appear, at the expense of others.'

Following his gaze, Georgiana stared at the charming little salon as if seeing it for the first time. The walls, painted in palest green, were a perfect foil for the soft colours of the Aubusson carpet. They threw into relief the graceful lines of her much prized furniture made of rosewood and mahogany by the hand of a master craftsman. A china cabinet in the corner held a collection of expensive *bibelots* and Sèvres porcelain.

As her eyes returned to her tormentor the small gold clock on the alabaster mantelshelf struck the hour of three.

'It did not occur to you to question the cost of all this luxury, or to ask how your brother could afford it?'

'Harry won large sums at White's,' she faltered.

'And lost more. Now let us have done with this charade. You will kindly inform me of your brother's whereabouts.'

Georgiana decided to play for time. 'I do not know you, sir, and your manner towards me has given me no cause to trust you.'

'Then allow me to introduce myself. I am Edward, Viscount Lyndhurst. I think you know my brother, Richard Thorpe.'

Georgiana's eyes grew wide. At the discovery of her visitor's identity she felt robbed of the power of speech.

Impatient now, the Viscount awaited her reply. Getting none, he seized her wrist again and his blue eyes hardened further.

'You will tell me, madam, I assure you.' The

deep voice was soft, but it held more menace than if he had shouted aloud. It terrified her.

'Let me go!' she cried in panic. She knew of the Viscount's reputation. According to his brother he was a ruthless tyrant who would stop at nothing to get his way. 'A cold fish', was the kindest description she had heard of him. Only during the Viscount's absence in the Indies had Richard enjoyed a respite from his cruelty.

As she raised her eyes to Lyndhurst's face she could believe his brother's words. Perhaps it was some trick of the light upon those aquiline features, or only the result of her overwrought imagination, but as he bent towards her he reminded her of some great bird of prey closing in upon his kill.

'You have heard of me, I see.' He laughed again, and it was not a pleasant sound. He had read her mind as easily as if she had spoken her thoughts aloud.

Gathering all her courage, Georgiana faced him squarely. 'Your treatment of your brother does you no credit. Your reputation has preceded you—but you shall not injure mine.'

'Others will do that, Miss Westleigh.' Lyndhurst glanced round the room again. 'You know, of course, that all your assets will be sequestered by the sheriff?'

'I…I don't know what you mean.'

'I mean that your home and its contents will be sold to pay your brother's creditors. By this time next week you could be turned out of doors with no roof above your head. What will you do?'

Georgiana felt as if the blood in her veins had turned to ice. Her heart began to thump unpleasantly, and nausea threatened to overwhelm her. She had given Harry her last few guineas, believing that the sale of their home and its contents would raise enough money to provide them with funds for a year or two. Now, it appeared, she would be penniless, and without even the means to travel to France.

'Doubtless it does not concern you,' the mocking voice continued. 'You are, perhaps, an heiress in your own right?'

The sarcasm cut Georgiana to the quick, but it had the opposite effect to that which the Viscount had intended. Her fear of him vanished. This time he had gone too far.

'Do you dare to call yourself a gentleman?' she enquired coolly. 'If so, I hope not to meet another such. You are insulting, sir. I am no heiress, but if there are debts they shall be settled. I do not care about possessions.'

'A praiseworthy sentiment, but foolhardy.'

The fierce eyes glared at her from beneath jutting brows. 'You do not expect me to believe you?'

'You think me a liar as well as a cheat?'

'Add fool to that assessment of your character and we shall agree. There is not a woman alive who does not prize material goods above all else. I give you that information on good authority.'

'You speak from experience, I suppose. Well, let us say, my lord, that in your own case material goods maybe all you have to offer. I have detected neither charm nor basic good manners.'

Lyndhurst's face grew dark with anger. For a second Georgiana quailed, but she would not retract her words. Then, to her surprise, he began to speak in a more reasonable tone.

'Quarrelling will serve no purpose, Miss Westleigh. Your worthy offer to settle your brother's debts is unrealistic. You will not raise above a thousand pounds under the hammer...a mere bagatelle in view of the sums involved. This was not explained to you?'

'N-no.' Georgiana's pallor had intensified.

A low curse escaped the Viscount's lips, but he continued his remorseless inquisition.

'You speak from ignorance when you disclaim

all interest in possessions. Do you know what it is like to be a vagrant, cold and hungry?'

'Do you?' she flung back at him.

'Thank God it has not been my lot, but I have seen enough of it. Enough to convince me of the need to be beforehand with the world.'

In spite of her dislike of him Georgiana was tempted to smile. That must be the understatement of all time. 'As rich as Croesus,' Richard had described his brother and as tight-fisted with his money as any shylock.

Lyndhurst began to pace the room.

'I asked what you would do, and you did not answer me. Can you return to your family home?'

Her silence was so prolonged that he gave her a curious look.

'Well?'

Long dark lashes veiled the green eyes, and Georgiana, to all appearances, was absorbed in studying the pattern on the carpet.

'That would be impossible,' she said at last. 'My father... Well, Harry is disowned... I was angry and I followed him. It was so unfair, you see.'

The silence intensified.

'I do see. The red hair does not lie, it would appear. Shall I add wilfulness to your other delightful qualities?' Lyndhurst answered slowly. He walked over to her, reached out, and allowed a gleaming copper strand to slide through his fingers. 'You are overly young to champion your brother's cause, I fear.'

'I am the elder,' Georgiana said with dignity. 'And pray, my lord, do not concern yourself with my affairs. I shall do very well without your advice.'

'At twenty...or can you be twenty-one? I doubt it.'

'My age can be of no possible interest to you, sir.'

Let him think what he liked. She would not give him the satisfaction of admitting that she was twenty-three.

He drew up a chair and sat down facing her.

'Come, let me make amends,' he said more gently. 'You have my sincere apologies for mistaking your status in this house, and I admire your loyalty. God knows, it is a quality rare enough in women—or men, for that matter. But do consider... These present difficulties are not easily resolved. They are beyond you.'

His voice was almost kind, and Georgiana ventured a look at his downcast head. Sensing her regard, he raised his eyes to hers and smiled. Georgiana's heart turned over. That smile transformed the harsh lines of his face. It lit up the room, warming her troubled soul and giving her the first crumbs of comfort she had known since Harry had told her the awful news of his ruin.

'Will you not trust me?' Lyndhurst continued. 'We may yet save something from the wreckage.'

Georgiana blinked away her tears. She could be brave when faced with anger, but the offer of help threatened to destroy her composure.

'I cannot help you,' she murmured. 'I have no resources. I can be of no use to you.'

'Nonsense! You have information. That is a resource to which I cannot lay claim. Will you share it with me?'

'I don't know. I must have time to think.'

'My dear, there *is* no time. You must see that. Now look at me! This may be your only chance to help your brother.'

A lean brown hand slid beneath her chin, tilting her face to his. Still irresolute, Georgiana looked deep into his eyes, and there she found the solution to the first, and most immediate, of her problems. The Viscount was clearly a man to whom the habit of command came easily. Nothing would be allowed to stand in his way, and with his help she would get to France.

'I will tell you,' she said at last. 'But there are two conditions. First, you must give me your word that you will not call my brother out.'

'That young puppy! What do you take me for? I might give him a whipping…'

'Then you will understand my second condition. When you follow them you must take me with you.'

The Viscount was on his feet at once.

'Impossible! I'll not be saddled with a weeping wench…'

'Thank you so much. Then I fear you must manage as best you may.'

'I beg your pardon, Miss Westleigh. Your suggestion startled me into impropriety. But you must see that it is out of the question.'

'Very well.' Georgiana sat with folded hands. 'You had best set about your enquiries, sir. You are wasting time.'

'How many times do I have to tell you? There *is* no time.' His voice was heavy with exasperation. 'Good God. Miss Westleigh, you can have no idea of the scandal caused by their hare-brained schemes. Are we to add to it?'

'You cannot be thinking of my reputation. A wilful, lying cheat can have no worries on that score.'

His look was inimical. 'Madam, I am thinking of my own. I have had one such experience. I would not willingly risk another.'

'Then there is no more to be said. I bid you goodnight, my lord.'

The Viscount glared at her.

'Blackmail, Miss Westleigh? I wonder why it should come as a surprise? You and your brother must deal famously together. The sooner my brother is removed from his influence, the easier I shall sleep at night.'

'Then you agree?'

'Have your way.' Lyndhurst turned away. 'You had best call your maid.'

'I have no maid.' Georgiana did not look at him. 'The servants were dismissed today.' She was fully prepared for the explosion of wrath which followed.

'Then how in heaven's name are you to travel? As my light-o'-love?'

'I am sure that no one would suspect you of such frivolous behaviour,' Georgiana taunted. She owed him that for his previous rudeness, and was pleased to notice the tightening of his lips. She gave him no time to reply. 'I had considered a more decorous role as your sister, or, perhaps, as your ward.'

'God forbid!' he said with feeling. 'In any case, no female relative of mine would travel without an abigail.'

'Then your tiger? My hair is short enough, in the style of Lady Caroline Lamb, and I am quite small.'

She had intended to shock him and she succeeded. He rounded on her with a look that boded ill.

'Are you out of your mind?' he asked in icy tones. 'Does your folly know no bounds? You would dare to set forth in breeches, madam? You shall not do so in my company.'

Georgiana's lips twitched, and he responded with a haughty look.

'I see. Is this some misplaced attempt to gammon me?'

'I should not dare, my lord.' Georgiana was at her most demure. 'I am in no joking mood, and did you not say yourself that time was of the essence?' She moved towards the door. 'I shall not keep you above a moment.'

'Stay!' For once he seemed nonplussed. 'No breeches, Miss Westleigh, I beg of you. You may travel as my ward.'

'That would seem to be the most appropriate solution, sir.'

His look was full of suspicion, and Georgiana was tempted to giggle. Perhaps he thought she was referring to age, or to his antiquated ideas. If so, she was glad of it. She had suffered enough from his barbed remarks.

What a prude he was! Stiff-backed, stiff-necked, and quite without the saving grace of humour. The journey ahead of her promised to be a trial in his company, but she would suffer it to reach Calais.

As she threw clothing into a bag her thoughts were sombre. Everything had happened so fast. Was it really less than forty-eight hours since Harry had returned ashen-faced to tell her that he was ruined?

Desperate, he had spent the previous day trying to raise funds, but all to no avail. She herself had pocketed her pride and applied to her own friends. They had given what they could, but the sums involved were too great. A fifty-guinea loan here and there went no way at all towards rescuing him from the consequences of his own folly, but she had taken the money with gratitude in order to help him.

She buried her face in her hands. She had intended to repay the money when the house was sold, but now she too would be labelled as a cheat. She rocked to and fro in an agony of mind. The future did not bear thinking of.

She jumped as the door flew open.

'This is no time for a fit of the vapours, Miss Westleigh.' The Viscount's voice was brisk. 'Make haste! We are wasting time.' He seized her bag and started down the stairs. 'Give me our destination. I must instruct my coachman.'

'I shall not tell you.' Georgiana gave him a defiant look. 'If you know it you will abandon me.'

Lyndhurst stared at her for a long moment.

'This may come as a surprise to you, but once I have given my word I keep it. Unlike your brother's assurances, you may rely upon that.' Without more ado he bundled her into the waiting coach.

'Well? I am waiting…' He sat back with an expression of saintly patience.

'We…we should make for the coast.'

'The coastline of England is extensive, Miss Westleigh. Shall we start in Cornwall and work our way around to the Scottish border?'

'Tell your man to make for Dover.' To discourage further conversation Georgiana drew her cloak about her and settled into the corner seat.

'So it is to be France?' her companion mused. 'And not a moment too soon, by the look of matters.'

'What do you mean?' Georgiana abandoned all pretence and sat bolt upright.

'Look there!' Lyndhurst drew aside the leather curtain at the window and nodded towards the corner of the street. Georgiana saw a group of men, dimly visible in the first pale light of dawn, making towards her door.

'So soon?' she breathed. 'Oh, please let us go.'

She did not look back, but as the coach rumbled away over the cobblestones she heard shouts and the sound of knocking.

'They will soon force the door,' the Viscount observed. 'I warned you, did I not? Now be good enough to tell me how the conspirators intended to travel.'

'I will tell you nothing if you persist in referring to my brother as if he were a criminal.'

'Fraud is a criminal offence, my dear. But if the term offends you I will rephrase my question. How do our unfortunate relatives intend to get away?'

'Lord Lothmore sent his chaise for Harry. He was to take it across the river, and there change into our own coach for the journey to Dover.'

'Doubtless collecting Richard on the way.

Damn Lothmore! When I spoke to him last evening he disclaimed all knowledge of Westleigh's whereabouts.'

'Perhaps he values loyalty,' Georgiana said stiffly.

'A quality which is sometimes sadly misplaced, Miss Westleigh.' His brow creased in thought. 'They will be forced to stop for a change of horses. We'll enquire at the post-houses.'

Tapping his gold-topped clouded cane against the roof, he brought the coach to a halt. A brief conference with his coachman ended with an injunction to 'Spring 'em!', and the horses gathered speed.

Chapter Two

Georgiana closed her eyes once more, but any attempt to sleep was out of the question.

With every jolt in the rutted road she was flung about. In vain she felt for a handhold in order to keep her balance, but a small scream escaped her lips as the coach hit a deep pothole and she was thrown into Lyndhurst's arms. Instinctively they closed about her, and he held her close for a moment.

She found the experience oddly disturbing, and for the first time she was aware of his immense strength. His arms might have been made of iron.

Knowing that it would be useless to struggle, she lay in his embrace, aware of the faint smell of tobacco mingled with that of expensive soap, and the lingering scent of salt sea air. The fine stuff of his coat felt smooth against her cheek, and beneath the ruffled shirt she could hear the beating of his heart.

He set her back in her corner with a mocking smile.

'Comfortable, Miss Westleigh?'

Georgiana felt too confused to reply. In silence she set her bonnet straight and shook out the folds of her warm merino cloak.

'Think how you'd have enjoyed the role of tiger,' he continued slyly. 'So bracing…riding aloft exposed to wind and rain.'

'It isn't raining, and if your coachman were not driving like a madman all would be well.' She gave him a bitter look.

'It can't be helped. We have no time to lose.'

Again the coach hit a pothole, and in an involuntary movement she put out her hands towards him. He laughed, but changed his seat at once to settle down beside her. A long arm slid about her waist and drew her close.

'You are too slight in weight,' he reproved. 'Were you twice the size you would not suffer so.'

'I need neither your help nor your advice,' Georgiana said with dignity. She sat bolt upright in the hope that he would move away. Instead he tightened his grip.

'My lord, you are crushing my gown.'

'Better that than a crushed nose! When I restore you to the arms of your loving brother I do not wish him to think that I have been beating you in my uncontrollable fury.'

'That is ridiculous!' Georgiana caught at his hand and tried to disengage his fingers from her waist, without success.

'Is it? I must confess that since we met I've been strongly tempted to beat you. Never in my experience have I encountered such a stubborn, feather-headed creature.'

A feeling of indignation almost robbed Georgiana of speech.

'I am *not* feather-headed!' she retorted in a choked voice.

'No? How else would you describe this present escapade?'

'What would you have had me do?' she cried bitterly. 'Should I have stayed in London to face the duns? You made it clear that they would turn me out of my home.'

'I hope I also made it clear that your most sensible course of action was to return to your parents.

However, we shall not dwell on it. We are thrown together, it would seem, for better or for worse.'

She was tempted to tell him that the worse, in her opinion, far outweighed the better, but she bit back the words. Lyndhurst was her only hope of getting to France, so she must make the best of what promised to be a nightmare journey.

It would be both useless and undignified to struggle further, so she allowed herself to grow limp within the circle of his arms and closed her eyes. She thought she heard a low chuckle, but she ignored it.

'That's better!' he murmured. 'I cannot have you looking as if you have been in the ring with Gentleman Jackson.'

'You have not heard me complain, nor will you.'

'That's true, but consider my difficulty. Should you strike your head and be rendered senseless I shall lose my guide. I shall not know whether to set sail for Bordeaux, La Rochelle, or Calais.' He felt her stiffen at the mention of Calais, but he made no comment.

'At our present rate of travel you will come upon your brother before we reach Dover,' she ground out.

'Possibly. But I doubt it. Our interesting relatives had too good a start on us.'

The sarcasm in his voice was hateful, and Georgiana turned her head away. Honesty compelled her to admit the truth of much of what he had said, and now, lying in his arms, she realised for the first time that she had placed herself in an invidious position.

It had been easy enough to defy him, and even to blackmail him into bringing her along, but there was no denying the fact that she was now in a closed carriage alone with a total stranger.

Her heart began to thump unpleasantly at the thought, but she forced herself to strive for calm. After all, it was clear that the Viscount had no high opinion of women. He had done his best to dissuade her from the journey, and he had been forthright about his opinion of her character.

She stole a glance at him from beneath lowered lids. Far from being aware of her presence he had closed his eyes, and was, to all appearances, falling asleep.

Georgiana smiled at her own fears. She was safe enough with this irritating creature. No woman would meet his exacting standards, least of all herself.

Idly, she found herself wondering about his past. He was unmarried; that she knew from Richard. It seemed strange that a man of his position should not have taken a wife and started his nursery. In spite of her dislike she would allow that he was an imposing figure. She glanced at him again, sure now that he was sound asleep.

She would not term him handsome…the face was too strong for conventional good looks. Those jutting brows, the Roman nose and the clean lines of a square jaw were oddly at variance with the thick mass of dark brown curls, dressed in the fashionable Brutus cut. To her own surprise she was tempted to touch a gleaming lock which had fallen across his forehead.

As if sensing her regard, the blue eyes opened wide.

'Having second thoughts, Miss Westleigh? Very wise! Give me your brother's destination and I'll set you down, with funds, at the first of the posthouses.'

Georgiana was sorely tempted. With funds she could make her own way to France, but a moment's thought convinced her not to accept his offer. She thought she knew her companion well enough to realise that he would not abandon her to her own devices. She decided to put him to the test.

'There are conditions?'

'Naturally! I cannot allow you to follow me to

France, having sent me off on some wild-goose chase. You will give me your word to return to your parents' home, by the coach which I shall order for you.'

'On no account!' Georgiana gave him a mutinous look.

'Very well! It shall be as you wish. I will take you to France...and then?'

Georgiana stared at him in dismay. She had not thought beyond the need to rush to Harry's side.

'My brother will obtain a post,' she faltered. 'He will take care of me.'

'As he has done to date? His tender care did not include taking you with him, I see.'

'That was my decision,' she retorted hotly. 'Harry did not wish to leave me, but I insisted. I thought...well, I thought that I might follow him when all was settled about the house in London.'

'What an innocent you are! Or did you hope to sell your possessions before your creditors could claim what was owed to them?'

Georgiana was silent. His words stung because there was so much truth in them. She *was* an innocent. In a blind panic, she had not stopped to think that everything she and Harry owned belonged, by rights, to his creditors. She had pressed her last few guineas on him, believing that she could raise enough money to follow him and enable them to live until he could find a position. She blushed furiously, feeling acutely uncomfortable.

'You will do well together,' the cynical voice continued. 'Are you to be the Judas goat, and lead the lambs to the slaughter? That look of innocence will serve for a year or two, but when the bloom wears off you will face an uncertain future, I assure you.'

Tears sprang unbidden to Georgiana's eyes. Must this unpleasant creature be so ready to put her own fears into words? She choked back a sob.

'Forgive me!' A large hand reached out to cover her own. 'That was unpardonable. I spoke in haste. Will you make allowances for my natural anger and anxiety?'

Georgiana dashed away a tear. She would not trust herself to speak, but she nodded briefly.

Obsessed by her own worries, she had given little thought to how Lyndhurst must be feeling. To return from a length absence to find his brother involved in scandal was bad enough, but the nature of that scandal made it insupportable. He had every right to feel betrayed by his brother's folly, but if only Harry were not involved...

She straightened her shoulders. Regrets were useless. Nothing she could say or do would alter what was past. She must learn to live for the day if she and Harry were to survive.

'Better?' The Viscount's voice was gentle. 'We are close to the first of the posthouses. We may have some news of them.'

His hopes were quickly realised. Mine host was happy to inform the Viscount that a coach bearing two young gentlemen of fashion had indeed passed through.

The landlord of the inn had good cause to remember them. More gold than he had seen in a twelve-month had accompanied a plea for haste in changing the horses. He had asked no questions. The change had been accomplished in record time, and the coach and its occupants would, by now, be some hours ahead of his lordship.

More gold changed hands, and Lyndhurst swung aboard with a request to his man for no slackening in speed.

'We shall not catch them before they reach Dover, unless they break a trace,' he frowned.

'Pray do not wish for that. They may be injured.'

'I think it unlikely. Those two young sprigs appear to bear charmed lives.' The Viscount's tone was grim. 'You have no idea how they mean to cross the Channel, I suppose? The packet will not take a coach without previous warning. Does your brother intend to leave it at the port?'

'Oh, no! He cannot. It contains all that Harry…I mean that we own in this world.'

'Then Westleigh was not unprepared for flight?'

'He took little enough,' Georgiana flared. 'And he was thinking of me rather than himself.'

'Was he indeed? I wish I had your faith in human nature.'

'Do you have faith in anything, or anyone?' Her look was hostile.

'Merely in a sense of honour and a modicum of intelligence,' he replied.

Georgiana was silenced. She was tired and stiff and in no mood for further exchanges with her unpleasant companion. Exhaustion overcame her at last, and even the constant rocking of the coach could not prevent her from falling asleep.

She awoke to the cries of sea-birds, and the unwelcome realisation that she was resting comfortably against the Viscount's broad shoulder. His chin was against her hair, and for a moment she thought that he too was asleep.

As she attempted to sit upright she found a pair

of keen blue eyes gazing down at her. As the coach drew to a halt he withdrew his arm from about her waist.

'We have reached Dover,' he announced. 'Though I fear we have missed our fugitives. They may have sailed on the morning tide. Will you excuse me? I must enquire for them.'

Once alone, Georgiana ran her fingers through her curls. Her merino cloak had stood the journey well, but her gown was crushed beyond redemption. What a fright she must look! She felt in her reticule for a mirror and a comb, groaning at her reflection in the glass. Dishevelled could scare describe it!

'No need to trouble yourself,' a calm voice observed from the window. 'Only the young look newborn in the morning light.'

It was a pretty compliment, but Lyndhurst's words brought her no comfort. Anxiously she scanned the crowds on the dockside, fearing to see Harry among the bustle of folk. She prayed that he had already sailed for France, and was out of her companion's reach.

She needed time to decide on her future course of action. Somehow she must contrive to mislead Lyndhurst. She dared not risk a confrontation with her brother. The Viscount had spoken of a whipping…

As she watched, he disappeared into an official-looking building, and was gone for so long that she began to fear the worst. She fervently hoped that Harry and Richard were not already taken.

She fixed her eyes on the doorway through which Lyndhurst had vanished, aware of an unpleasant churning in her stomach. Her heart was pounding, and she sensed a curious fluttering in her breast.

Clenching her fists until the knuckles shone white, she forced herself to breathe deeply until the fluttering stopped. She must be calm. To panic would serve no purpose. Above all she needed a clear head if she was to outwit her dangerous companion.

When he reappeared his expression was not encouraging.

'We are too late,' he told her briefly. 'They are gone.'

Inwardly, Georgiana sighed with relief. Harry was safe for the moment, and out of reach of possible pursuers. She looked up at the Viscount with dancing eyes.

Her joy was short-lived. He left her in no doubt of his intentions.

'We shall find them,' he said with certainty. 'Now, Miss Westleigh, to business. We cannot sail until tonight, so I suggest that we break our fast. You will wish to retire to make a toilette, and you must be famished.'

'I could not eat.' At that moment Georgiana felt that food would choke her.

'Yet you will do so. I'll not be burdened by a fainting female…'

Argument died on her lips as she looked at his stern expression, but he had not done with her.

'The sea is looking ugly,' he went on. 'You will find that retching is most unpleasant on an empty stomach.' He sounded as if the thought gave him a great deal of pleasure.

'I am an excellent sailor, thank you,' Georgiana said with dignity.

'You will have need to be.' He did not speak to her again until they entered the portals of the largest inn in the town.

The Viscount's manner was such that no trace of surprise was permitted to appear on the face of mine host, no matter what his private conjecture as to the likely relationship of his guests. If the lady had no attendant and very little luggage it was none of his concern.

A glance at the perfect set of the coat across the Viscount's broad shoulders, the magnificence of his tasselled Hessians, and the fine quality of his snowy linen, assured the man that he was dealing with the Quality. Not that he needed further assurance. He had seen the coach arrive, noted the crested panelling on the doors, and was unsurprised to find that the habit of command came easily to his visitor.

If the lady looked overly young and not a little nervous, it was to be understood. This would not be the first time that some dashing buck had brought a barque of frailty to the shelter of his roof.

'Your room has a private parlour,' the Viscount murmured. 'Wait for me there. I have some matters to attend, but I shall not be long. Have you any preference in the matter of food?'

'Anything. It does not matter.' Georgiana felt uncomfortable. She had not misinterpreted the landlord's bland expression.

'On the contrary! It matters to me.' Lyndhurst turned away, apparently dismissing her from his thoughts.

He was gone for longer than she expected, leaving her a prey to dread. In spite of his promise he might still abandon her without compunction. She had turned down his generous offer of funds and a coach. Perhaps he felt that he owed her nothing further. Now that he knew Harry's destination, why should he not leave her to her fate? At Calais he could search for the fugitives with every hope of success. The town was not large...

She pushed her worrying thoughts to the back of her mind, but niggling doubts remained. Should he not return, this well-furnished bedchamber with its private parlour was well beyond her means. She would be hard-pressed to mollify the landlord, and how could she pay for a passage to France?

Until this moment she had not realised how dependent she was upon the Viscount's protection. A frown creased her brow. With an impatient gesture she rose to her feet and began to pace the room.

She would not meet trouble halfway. By this time tomorrow she would be in France. She must believe that Lyndhurst was a man of his word, and in her heart she was sure of it. She disliked him, it was true. His intimidating manner and his cruel tongue were not designed to charm, but then, she had no claim upon his forbearance.

He thought her some kind of an adventuress...certainly a liar and a cheat. Her cheeks burned as she recalled his words. It should not matter what he thought of her, but it was hard to be misjudged. She found herself wondering what his reaction would have been had they met under other circumstances.

She pulled a face at herself in the mirror. The jade-green eyes, framed with long, dark lashes, mocked her gently. They were tip-tilted at the corners, giving her heart-shaped face a slightly feline appearance. As a child she had been nicknamed 'Puss', and she had learned to dislike that slanting gaze.

Her mouth she considered too wide for beauty. In any case, those flaming curls must quash all pretension to good looks. Blondes and brunettes were all the rage. Georgiana sighed for the fashion of fifty years ago, when hair had been powdered, but it would not have helped. A pair of arching eyebrows, dark as a raven's wing, would have ruined the effect.

She was an oddity, and, as such, the Viscount would have passed her by without a second glance. Her cheeks grew rosy as she considered the direction of her thoughts, but honesty compelled her to admit that she would prefer him to think well of her, if not exactly to be attracted to her appearance. He was a provoking creature, but she could not bear his contempt.

She walked over to the window, hoping to cool her flaming cheeks. The throng in the courtyard below milled about the London coach, which had just arrived. As she watched, the tall figure of the Viscount forced its way through the crowd to greet an elderly man dressed in sombre clothing.

Her sense of relief was overwhelming as she saw the two men enter the inn. Lyndhurst had kept his word as, in her heart, she had known he would. She felt ashamed of her doubts. If only there were some way she could mitigate his anger, justified though it was.

With a sigh she walked through into the private parlour. It was empty although a table had been laid with gleaming silver and glass. An appetising smell of roasting meat floated towards her from below, and suddenly she felt hungry.

She had not long to wait. Seconds later Lyndhurst entered the room. As she looked up, she surprised a curious expression on his face. In another man she might have thought it admiration.

Suddenly she was glad that she had chosen to wear her most becoming gown. Classical in line, the filmy fabric, in palest green, was caught high beneath her bosom with an emerald ribbon. It had been sadly crushed, but she'd held it over a bowl of steaming water to remove the creases. Now she smoothed at it with nervous fingers.

The Viscount did not appear to notice her confusion. With grave courtesy he seated her at the table, and motioned to the waiting servants. They sat in silence as the meal was served and the landlord himself carved thin pink slices of the tender ham in Madeira sauce which followed a delicious fish soup.

The Viscount had a healthy appetite and did full justice to the haunch of mutton which then appeared, raising an eyebrow as Georgiana refused an offer of beef with caramelised onions. Instead she took a serving of young salad greens.

'You have not touched your wine,' Lyndhurst said at last. 'It is not to your taste?'

Georgiana sipped from her glass.

'It is very good, my lord.'

He smiled then and she bridled, knowing full well that he suspected her of caution. He was right. She was not used to taking more than a glass, and she feared that the wine might loosen her tongue.

'At least you will try this mint and lemon ice, madam?' the landlord pleaded. 'Or perhaps a mouthful of this soufflé? It is as light as air.'

Georgiana smiled and shook her head, and Lyndhurst signalled to the man to withdraw.

'I have hired a vessel,' he announced when they were alone. 'We leave on the evening tide.'

Georgiana's heart lifted. At least he did not intend to leave her behind. He gave her a speculative look. 'By tomorrow we shall be in Calais…' He seemed to be waiting for some comment.

'And then?' she breathed.

'Why, then we shall trace our missing relatives, of course.'

'I did not mean quite that. My lord, you have not said what you intend to do if…when we find them.'

'Let us take one day at a time.' His expression was bland. 'Have you everything you need for the journey? Do you wish to go into the town…?'

'I have sufficient for my needs,' she said stiffly. She would not be further beholden to him, but it was an ungracious reply, and she coloured a little. 'It is kind of you to think of it, and I thank you.'

'You will thank me best by getting some sleep.' His face had closed again and his voice was distant.

Georgiana wondered why a simple word of thanks should have annoyed him so. His courtesy had disarmed her, and for a moment she had been in danger of forgetting that she was nothing more to him than a link with Harry.

She had been fed and cared for because she was of use to him, yet she had been foolish enough to imagine that concern for her had prompted his kindness. An irrational wave of anger tempted her to lash out at him. She would not make the same mistake again.

Then common sense prevailed. There was no point in making an enemy of him at the present time. She needed him as much as he needed her, and until now she had handled matters badly. Perhaps if she tried a different approach...?

'You are right, of course.' She gave him her sweetest smile. 'May I thank you first for an excellent meal?' She sat back with a sigh of contentment, and was disconcerted to see that his wide, mobile mouth was twisted in amusement.

'You feel quite well, Miss Westleigh?'

'Why should I not?'

'I thought I detected a certain softening in your manner, yet you refused my offer of a visit to the shops to replenish your wardrobe.'

'I have no need of anything, as I told you.'

'Not even a pair of breeches? I imagined that you might be considering another role...as my cabin-boy.' He gave her a malicious grin.

Georgiana stared at him in amazement. A joke from Lyndhurst? Was he actually teasing her? She struggled to repress a smile.

'You are pleased to jest,' she said sedately. 'Now if you will excuse me I shall retire.'

A cool hand reached out to rest upon her brow.

'What are you doing?' She pulled away from him.

'I suspect a violent fever. When you fall in with my wishes I fear the worst.'

Georgiana glared at him. A sharp retort rose to her lips, but she held her tongue. With head held high, she swept from the room.

Chapter Three

The day was far advanced when she awoke, and for a few moments she wondered where she was. A movement in the corner roused her, and she lifted her head to find a girl of her own age regarding her with interest.

'Who are you…and what are you doing here?' Georgiana raised herself on one elbow.

'Beg pardon, madam. His lordship asked me to see toy our things. I've pressed your gowns.'

'You work here?'

'No, ma'am. My uncle is his lordship's valet. We came down on the London coach.'

Lyndhurst had not wasted much time, Georgiana thought wryly. He must have sent a message to his servants from the first of the posthouses on the Dover road. Had he taken any other action unknown to her? If he had notified the authorities...

Then she remembered. Harry and Richard were out of reach of the Bow Street Runners.

Throwing aside the coverlet, she slipped out of bed, glad to find that the girl had laid out a change of clothing.

'What is your name?' she asked.

'I'm Betsy, ma'am. Shall I ring for hot water?'

'Please.' Georgiana smiled at her. The girl was small and thin, but she was clearly anxious to be helpful, and she had a pleasant face. 'Do you go to France with us?'

'Yes, miss. I'm afeared of the sea, but my uncle says it will be all right.'

'Of course it will. You have not travelled to France before?'

Betsy giggled. 'I ain't bin above three mile from home afore now, but I'm to train as a lady's maid. His lordship promised.'

'It won't be difficult,' Georgiana murmured. 'Now if you will find my stout half-boots...'

Leaving the girl to rummage through her bag, she abandoned herself to the luxury of a bath in warm, scented water.

'Miss, I was to tell his lordship once you was awake,' Betsy offered hesitantly.

'Very well, but first you shall help me into my gown.'

The girl was both clumsy and nervous, but her hands were gentle, if a trifle impatient. Georgiana guessed that, for his servants, Lyndhurst's word was law and, by waiting, Betsy was disobeying his express command.

'Off you go!' She released the girl at last. 'I will do my hair myself.'

Betsy gave her a look of pure gratitude as she hurried away, but she was back at once.

'I'm to help you with your hair.' There was a note of pride in the girl's voice.

Georgiana hid a smile. 'It will not take long,' she said gravely. 'As you see, it is very short.'

She sat patiently as Betsy brushed at her curls.

'It's that springy, ma'am, but it's beautiful.' Betsy touched the flaming mass with reverence. 'Ain't you lucky to have dark brows? Most folk with red hair look like frightened rabbits.'

Georgiana's shoulders shook. Betsy promised to be a most unusual lady's maid, and vastly entertaining.

She dismissed the girl and strolled into the parlour to find it deserted, but in the courtyard below the bustle had not lessened. As she gazed across the rooftops of the little town she could see ships at anchor in the harbour below. Which of them would bear her to France? And, once there, what was to be her fate?

She turned as the door opened. As the Viscount sauntered towards her his manner was as cool as ever, but to her surprise he took her hand and kissed it in greeting. The touch of his warm lips against her skin was strangely disturbing, but she resisted the temptation to betray her unease by snatching it away. After all, the greeting was no more than common courtesy. Frayed nerves must have caused that curious little flicker in the pit of her stomach.

With all the composure at her command, she looked up at him and smiled. She had sworn to herself that she would not antagonise him further, or her plan to persuade him to trust her must fail.

Honesty compelled her to admit that his appearance was a tribute both to his own physique and to the attentions of his valet. The snowy starched cravat was creased to perfection à la Mathématique, and his dark brown hair gleamed in the sunlight streaming through the window. It shone like a newly fallen chestnut. The fit of his coat and breeches bespoke the hand of a master tailor, and no speck of dust marred the surface of his tasselled Hessians.

She felt a small pang of regret. His was a striking figure, though his dress was understated. Anyone unversed in the finer points of style would have found it unremarkable at first glance, but she had been well trained by Harry. How often had she listened to her brother's lamentations as he struggled to achieve a similar standard?

This man was no dandy, but he looked every inch an aristocrat. She sighed outwardly. Under other circumstances she might have found Lyndhurst pleasing.

She turned away, banishing the treacherous thought.

'You are rested?'

'Yes, my lord.'

'Then you are ready to face the rigours of a Channel crossing?'

'Quite ready!' Belatedly, she remembered Betsy. 'I must thank you for sending a maid to me.'

She heard a chuckle.

'It may be some time before Betsy can claim that title. You find her willing enough?'

Georgiana dimpled, and her mouth curved in a smile.

'May I not share the joke?'

'Betsy is pleased because I have dark brows and lashes,' she replied. 'Without them I should most certainly look like a frightened rabbit.'

Lyndhurst's twinkling eyes belied his frown.

'You must not brook impertinence. I will ask Scroggins to speak to her.'

'Please don't! I should not have told you had I thought you would take it amiss. Betsy is a joy.'

'You are easily pleased, Miss Westleigh. Now will you sit down? I have something to say to you.'

With no great hopes that it would be anything she wished to hear, Georgiana sank into a chair as her companion began to pace the room.

'I must make a last appeal to your good sense,' he said at last. 'Your present plans are folly. Will you not reconsider? My man and Betsy will accompany you to your parents' home.'

'Impossible!' Georgiana stiffened and her mouth set in a mutinous line.

'Why so? Sisterly affection may be excused. Your father will forgive you for championing your brother's cause.'

'No!'

'I find your attitude beyond all reason.' Lyndhurst was growing impatient. 'Your decision to live with Westleigh should not have been allowed. Your father, after all, has some claim upon your obedience.'

Hot colour flooded Georgiana's cheeks. She had no wish to offer an explanation to this authoritarian creature, but she had no alternative.

'My father did not know...of my whereabouts...'

The Viscount's eyebrows rose in disbelief, and his frown deepened.

'I...er...allowed everyone to think that I had eloped...'

'Indeed!' Lyndhurst's tone was grim. 'You had best go on.'

'Oh, don't you see?' she pleaded. 'It was the only way. Had Father found us he would have forced me to leave Harry. If he believed me to be married he could not interfere...'

'You have a curious idea of filial affection.' The contempt in Lyndhurst's voice made Georgiana squirm. 'Had you no thought for the distress you must have caused?'

'I did think of it,' she flung back furiously. 'I wrote to reassure my mother, but, of course, I could not tell her the truth.'

'Naturally not,' he agreed in an icy tone. 'At lease you have succeeded in confirming my opinion of you. Once a cheat…'

'How dare you?' she cried. 'Again you judge me without knowing the full story.'

'Then you had best tell me,' he said, with an unpleasant smile. 'As always, your beloved brother appears to be the cause of this separation from your family. He was disowned, I think you said. What had he done to warrant such a fate?'

Georgiana was silent as she glared at him. She would not discuss private family matters with this autocratic creature.

'I can find out, you know.' His lordship took a leisurely pinch of snuff. 'And you might remember that you cannot sink your brother's reputation further in my eyes. That would be impossible.'

'Really?' She faced him then with flashing eyes. 'You shall hear the story, sir. Then you may judge.'

'Go on.'

Georgiana hesitated. She was wondering where to begin. 'Harry was at Cambridge,' she muttered at last. 'He was sent down…'

'Why?'

'He was rather wild…and…and there were gambling debts…' She looked up at Lyndhurst, hating the mocking smile which played about his mouth. 'He was just a boy,' she snapped furiously. 'And whatever he had done it did not warrant…'

Her voice shook and she could not go on. The memory of her father's anger would live in her mind forever. She had not spoken of his behaviour to a living soul until this day.

'This was the cause of your father's displeasure?'

'Displeasure? That is a masterpiece of under-statement. My father is a violent man, my lord. He thrashed Harry with his riding crop before our friends and all the servants…'

'A father has the right to chastise his children.'

'To the point of breaking their bones? Harry put up an arm to save his head, but it did not stop the attack. We heard the crack as his arm snapped. My mother was weeping… She tried to stop the punishment but she was thrust away so fiercely that she fell to the ground. Then I…I seized the whip and threw it in the lake.'

'I see.' Lyndhurst's eyes were intent upon her face.

'Do you? I doubt if you can understand… Things were said that day which cannot be forgot-ten or forgiven.'

'By Harry?'

'Harry could not speak. He tried to crawl away, but my father told him to stand up and take his beating like a man. He picked up a stick of ash-plant, but my mother caught his arm whilst Harry's friends carried him to the surgeon. Father followed them down the drive, still screaming abuse…'

'My dear!' Lyndhurst's voice was gentler than she had heard it for some time. 'What of yourself?'

'I was beaten too, but with a cane.' She gave him a twisted smile. 'Then I was locked in my room for several days. Harry came back just once, to see my mother. Father ordered him out of the house. He said that he had no son. Harry begged to be allowed to say farewell to me, but permission was refused. My mother told me later that Harry had told my father that he would never forgive him.'

'And you?'

'Never! His treatment of Harry was beyond all reason. His anger I could understand…but not the brutality. Later I suppose he was ashamed, but he would not admit it. He hinted of other matters to his friends, saying that he could not bring himself to speak of the true cause of Harry's banishment.'

'Do you know of anything more?'

'There was nothing. Mother made it her business to find out from friends at Cambridge.'

'It must have been hard for you.'

'I was released in time.' Her smile was pitiful. 'But it was too late. I could not stay beneath my father's roof, and I had been given the opportunity to think. A week on bread and water does much to clear the mind. I rode over to see a friend of ours who was leaving for the colonies. He did not object when I told him of my plan.'

'Which was?'

'To say that we had eloped. He was emigrating and could not be traced with ease, at least for a time.'

'A gallant gentleman!' Lyndhurst's voice was dry. 'You had a *tendre* for him?'

'Not in the least!' Georgiana gave him a withering look. 'But he had no love for my father. When he asked for leave to pay his addresses to me, his suit was dismissed in the most insulting way.'

'And he did not renew it when he knew that you wished to leave your home?'

'He did.' Georgiana coloured faintly. 'But I explained that I could not marry him. In the end, he agreed to help me. We travelled to London with his sister and found Harry.'

'And your mother?'

'That is my only regret.' Her lips quivered. 'I left a note…and later I wrote to reassure her about

Harry and myself, but I do not know if she received the letter. My father may have destroyed it...'

'So you are adamant? There is no possibility of a reconciliation?'

'How can you ask?' Her eyes were bright with unshed tears. 'I cannot and will not return home. My lord, you gave me your word that I should accompany you to France, and I believed you.'

'You may live to regret it.' His face was sombre. 'You have my sympathy, Miss Westleigh. I was too hard on you, but I could wish that you had accepted your friend in marriage. It would have solved many of your problems.'

'And created more. I did not love him, and besides, no man shall master me. I had rather die a spinster.'

'Someone must control that stubborn will.' The fierce blue eyes raked her from head to foot with such an insolent look of appraisal that Georgiana felt naked beneath his gaze. 'And I doubt that you will die a spinster. That face and form will save you from such a fate.'

'You are no gentleman to speak so.' She blinked away the tears from her eyes. 'If you think to dissuade me with your insults you will not succeed.'

'Insults, my dear Miss Westleigh? Most women

would regard my tribute to your beauty as a compliment. However, I must point out that beauty in itself can be a handicap. You would travel to France alone with me? Have you no thought of your reputation?'

'My reputation is already lost. You have made that clear. I must bear the taint of scandal equally with my brother, as you were quick to tell me. To travel as your…companion cannot matter now.'

'Be it on your own head.' He turned and left her.

A chill wind was blowing by the time they reached the dock, and Georgiana looked in dismay at the leaden waves. The seas were mountainous.

'Miss, we shall be drownded for sure!' Betsy's eyes were starting from her head.

'Nonsense!' Georgiana spoke with a confidence she was far from feeling. 'The captain will not sail if there is danger.'

The keen wind cut through her warm merino cloak as if it were made of paper, and she looked in concern at her maid's thin garments. The girl was shaking, as much with cold as with fright.

'My lord?' Georgiana turned to the Viscount, who was supervising the loading of his coach aboard the waiting vessel.

'What is it now?' Lyndhurst was apparently oblivious of the inclement weather.

'May we not go aboard at once? You will not wish to have two fainting females on your hands.'

The taunt brought a tightening of his lips, but he nodded his assent. 'Scroggins will show you to your cabin.' A motion of his head brought the valet to their side, but it was with some trepidation that Georgiana stepped up the companionway.

The weather was atrocious, and, even tied up alongside, the ship was pitching unpleasantly. Georgiana remembered her own claim to be an excellent sailor. She hoped it would be justified.

To her relief the cabin was warm and comfortable, and Scroggins was attentive. He took his niece aside to give her further instructions, but Betsy paid him no attention. Her face was ashen, and before they were under way it had taken on a greenish tinge.

'You had best lie down,' Georgiana suggested. 'Then you will find the motion less disturbing.' She gestured towards the bunk.

'My uncle will be cross with me.' Tears poured down Betsy's cheeks. 'I wasn't to be a trouble to you but, miss, I do feel bad.'

'You will be more trouble if you are ill. Now do

as I say.' Georgiana tucked the girl beneath the coverlet. 'You must try to sleep. In no time at all we shall be in France, and on dry land again.'

She waited until the girl had closed her eyes, and then she left the cabin. Her appearance on deck was not welcomed by the Viscount. He gave her an angry look.

'This will not be an easy crossing,' he announced. 'I prefer that you stay below decks.'

'And I prefer fresh air.' Georgiana was finding it difficult to keep her footing in the gale, but she would not admit defeat.

'As you wish, my self-willed friend. A word of warning, though... If you are swept overboard I shall not attempt to save you.'

'Of course not! Such self-sacrifice would be totally out of character.' The effect of the barbed taunt was lost as the ship pitched into the trough of a wave and Georgiana lost her footing on the slippery deck. With a cry she threw out a hand to save herself.

'Now will you need my warning?' A grip of iron encircled her waist as the Viscount held her close. 'You had best seek your cabin.'

Still gasping with shock, Georgiana lifted her head. She had not allowed for the fury of the storm.

The force of the wind had almost thrown her off her feet. Mutely, she nodded, though she doubted if she had the strength to retrace her steps.

Lyndhurst solved the problem by picking her up and tossing her over one shoulder as if she had been a sack of feathers. Then he groped along the deck until they reached the safety of the companionway.

'Please set me down here.' It was difficult to maintain any semblance of dignity with her heels in the air, her bonnet askew, and her head and arms scrabbling vainly at the Viscount's back, but Georgiana did her best.

She might have saved her breath. Ignoring her pleas, he marched along to her cabin door, threw it open, and dumped her on a chair.

'Madam,' he said heavily, 'my patience has been sorely tried. You will oblige me by showing some consideration for your own welfare, if not for mine. It is a long swim back to Dover, even for a woman of your determination.'

Georgiana was pinned in her chair as he leaned towards her. His face was much too close and she shifted uncomfortably, averting her head. The lips which had been close to her ear now brushed her cheek, and she jumped as if she had been stung.

The intimate contact had discomfited Lyndhurst too, she realised. He straightened at once.

'I beg your pardon,' he said stiffly. A slight flush appeared beneath his tan. 'I did not mean…'

A silence fell between them, and the air was heavy with tension. It was unnerving, and Georgiana's mouth grew dry. Her every sense was aware of the man in front of her…his breathing…the smooth firmness of his skin…and the beautifully moulded mouth. How safe she had felt in his embrace, yet it was meaningless. He had reached out to her merely to save her from harm.

What would it be like to have him reach out for her in love, drawing her gently to him to share untold delights?

Her eyes grew soft as she looked into his own but his expression checked her. His face was cold and distant. He bowed and was about to leave her when retching noises from the bed confirmed that Betsy was in the throes of nausea.

'I'll get Scroggins,' he said quickly.

'No!' With swift fingers Georgiana unfastened her cloak. 'Betsy will not wish her uncle to know that she is unwell.' The ghost of a smile touched her lips. 'She was not to be a trouble to me, or to fail in her duty.'

The Viscount hesitated. 'Miss Westleigh, there is no necessity for you to undertake the duties of a nurse.' The cool formality of his tone succeeded in annoying Georgiana.

'For heaven's sake,' she cried impatiently. 'The girl is feeling wretched. Can't you forget your precious code for once?'

She had expected an explosion of wrath, but none was forthcoming.

'Leave us, please,' she cried. 'Your presence can only add to Betsy's discomfort.'

'Is there anything I can do?'

'You may send for cloths and a bowl of water.'

When she looked round she was alone except for the groaning girl on the bed.

Murmuring words of comfort, Georgiana bathed the pale, sweating face. Then she wedged herself into the corner beside the bunk and held on to Betsy's hand. She was feeling none too good herself.

With grim determination she gritted her teeth. She would not succumb to sickness. It was all in the mind, so Harry had told her, but half an hour later she had begun to doubt his words. Perhaps if she kept her head quite still the rolling motion would not trouble her so.

Between the crashing of the waves and the high keening of the wind she did not hear a tap at the door. She looked up in surprise as Lyndhurst entered the cabin.

'Try sucking this!' One look at her face had told him all he wished to know. 'This is a bad crossing, Miss Westleigh. You should lie down.' He handed her the two halves of a cut lemon.

'I… I don't think I could put anything in my mouth.' Georgiana closed her eyes to shut out the sight of the fruit.

'The sharpness will help,' he insisted.

Obediently she lifted the lemon to her lips, preventing herself from vomiting by an act of will.

'Since Betsy is asleep you may use my cabin.' It was an order rather than suggestion, and Georgiana made no demur as he picked her up.

She was feeling too wretched to resist as he laid her upon his bunk.

'Do you wish to loosen your clothing? You will be more comfortable…'

'I wish that the ship would sink,' she groaned. 'Please go away.'

'In a moment.' With hands that were surprisingly gentle he removed her half-boots and tucked the coverlet round her.

'Try to sleep,' he murmured. 'The storm is abating, and the wind is dropping. I believe we are over the worst.'

With these words of comfort he left her. As always, he proved to be right. Within minutes Georgiana sensed that the roll of the vessel was less pronounced. Even the wind had ceased its screaming through the rigging. She closed her eyes and slept.

The ship was at anchor when she awoke, and it was with relief that she heard the clatter of horses' hooves on cobblestones. Beyond the open porthole she was aware of chattering in a foreign tongue. They must be at Calais unless the ship had been blown off course. Wherever they were it was a safe landfall, for which she could only offer up her thanks to the Almighty.

'His lordship presents his compliments, madam.' Scroggins entered with a tray of freshly baked rolls, some fruit and a pot of coffee. 'He begs that you will join him at your earliest convenience.'

The valet's lips were set in a thin line, and Georgiana pulled a face at his retreating back. Every line of his body betrayed a sense of outrage at her behaviour.

'How is Betsy?' she asked quickly.

'My niece is recovered, I thank you. Had madam only thought to send for me, any disturbance might have been avoided.'

'How kind of you to consider my comfort, Scroggins.' Georgiana gave him a deliberate look. He knew, and so did she, that his concern had been not for her but for his master. So the Viscount was not to be turned out of his own cabin for a whim of hers?

The man's eyes fell. He bowed and took his leave. He had not even thanked her for her care of Betsy, she thought ruefully. Lyndhurst, it seemed, was the pivot of his existence.

She shrugged. It was a pity to make an enemy of the Viscount's servant, but it was not of her doing. Doubtless Scroggins regarded her as some lightskirt who had fallen in Lyndhurst's way and would soon be discarded. The man was as stiff-necked and prudish as his master, she thought in disgust. They made a perfect pair.

She knew that she was being unjust. To be quite fair, it was as well for her that Lyndhurst was blessed with iron self-control. He was a man with the same needs as others, and it could not be denied that she was at his mercy.

Last night, for example, he might have taken advantage of her. She had been in no fit state to oppose him, and they had been in this cabin alone.

The humour of the situation struck her. What man would attempt to seduce a woman who was clearly in the throes of *mal de mer?* Such an incautious move might have resulted in the ruin of his fine linen shirt, and those spotless buckskin breeches. She had certainly been looking her worst, and her groans had been no invitation to a night of passionate love.

With a chuckle she threw aside the coverlet and stood before a dressing mirror. The long sleep had refreshed her and her milky skin had lost its greenish tinge. She poured out her coffee and began to nibble at a roll. How good it tasted! She was halfway through a second when Betsy tapped at the cabin door.

'Miss, his lordship wondered if you was ready to go ashore.' The girl looked subdued, and her eyes were red.

Georgiana felt indignant. Had Scroggins berated her? It seemed more than likely. Lyndhurst would not have troubled himself to take her maid to task.

She was tempted to summon the man, but a moment's reflection convinced her that she might do more harm than good by confronting him directly. Doubtless Scroggins' unreasonable behaviour was influenced by that of his master. What an example for anyone to follow!

She laid a sympathetic hand on Betsy's shoulder.

'Are you feeling better?' she enquired.

Betsy nodded, struggling with her tears.

'I'm that sorry, miss,' she choked out at last. 'I didn't mean to turn you out of your bed...'

'It did not signify. I was quite comfortable in here.'

'Yes, but his lordship... Oh miss, my uncle is so cross with me...'

And with me, Georgiana thought to herself. But Scroggins would learn that he had met his match. It was time to change the subject.

'Help me to dress,' she said quickly. 'And cheer up, Betsy. We shall find the best cure in the world for seasickness.'

'What's that, madam?'

'Sitting under a tree,' Georgiana twinkled.

Betsy stared at her. 'I don't understand.' Then her face cleared as Georgiana smiled, and she began to laugh. 'Miss, you are a caution. I can't feel seasick on the land, can I?'

She was still grinning as she slipped a gown of

primrose-yellow cambric over Georgiana's head, but the smile vanished with the sound of knocking at the cabin door.

'May I come in?' Lyndhurst stood in the doorway. With a wave of his hand he motioned Betsy out of the room. 'I believe I mentioned the need for haste, Miss Westleigh. How much longer do you intend to keep me waiting?'

'Longer than if you had not dismissed my maid.' Georgiana's temper rose to match his own.

'She is here to dress you rather than to provide you with amusement,' came the cool reply.

So he had heard them laughing and resented it. What an unpleasant creature he was!

'I am ready.' She seized her cloak, and was about to sweep past him when she recalled his kindness on the previous night. Possibly he had had no sleep, she realised, which might account for his ill humour.

'I thank you for allowing me to use your cabin,' she said stiffly.

Lyndhurst ignored the olive branch.

'I am still waiting, madam. At this rate it will be noon before we disembark.'

Georgiana threw up her eyes to heaven. He was impossible! How she longed for the moment when she could slip away from him. If she never saw him again it would be too soon, but he had served her purpose. She was now in France, and she felt a surge of relief. What a joy it would be to see Harry again!

With a light step she moved towards the door, but as she passed Lyndhurst he swung her round to face him.

'You are in great good humour today, my dear.' The keen eyes scanned her face.

'I am thankful that the sea crossing is behind us, sir.' Long, dark lashes veiled Georgiana's eyes. 'I should not care to repeat that experience.'

'Did you not tell me that you were an excellent sailor?' he challenged.

The sarcasm in his voice was infuriating. Georgiana did not reply. Then a strong hand gripped her chin and lifted her face to his.

'No tricks, madam! Allow me to warn you that if you have any thought of deceiving me you will regret it.'

'Let me go!' She slapped his hand away from her face. 'How dare you touch me?'

He smiled then, but his eyes were cold, and suddenly Georgiana was afraid.

'You presume too much upon my goodwill, Miss Westleigh. I might have seduced you at any time since our first meeting. Do you think I am made of stone?'

Hot colour flooded Georgiana's cheek. 'You would not,' she cried wildly.

'Why not? Your character leaves much to be desired, but your face and figure does not. A man might enjoy those attributes, at least.'

'You are disgusting!' she flung at him.

'But you are not.' Swiftly he bent his head and claimed her lips. She struggled to turn away, but the firm mouth came down on hers, forcing her lips apart. As his tongue caressed her Georgiana felt a curious sensation in the pit of her stomach, and the urge to draw him even closer was overwhelming. Confusion warred with delight as she melted into his arms.

Her pleasure was short-lived. With a muttered exclamation he thrust her away, and bustled her out of the cabin. Once on deck he strode away as if the fiends of hell were at his heels.

Chapter Four

Bewildered and deeply shaken, Georgiana followed the tall figure of the Viscount as he made his way down the gangplank. Once ashore he did not look at her, leaving Scroggins to help her aboard the waiting coach.

Lyndhurst, she noted, had taken his seat aloft beside the coachman. She might have been a leper, she thought with a surge of indignation. After all, she had not encouraged him to take her in his arms.

Her face burned as she remembered the warmth of his lips against her mouth. Had she only imagined the passion which had flared between them? Whether it was true or not, it appeared to have given that infuriating creature a strong distaste for her company.

Perhaps it was as well. This was no time to fall in love with him, and she had no intention of doing so. She composed her features into a smooth mask of indifference, oblivious to a searching look from Scroggins, who occupied the facing seat. Betsy sat beside him, looking subdued.

Georgiana felt a rising tide of irritation. She was tired of both Lyndhurst and his sour-faced valet. Enough was enough. With a brilliant smile she addressed herself to Betsy.

'Well, we are here in France at last, my dear. Now we may start to enjoy ourselves.' A sly look at Scroggins showed her that the man had stiffened. His lips were compressed, but he did not speak.

'You must make the most of your visit here,' Georgiana continued brightly.

She affected not to notice the girl's nervous look at her uncle before she muttered her agreement. Had he threatened to send her back to England? She would put a stop to his threats at once.

'Scroggins, I doubt if I have expressed my thanks for bringing Betsy to me. I can't think how I should go on without her...'

'Madam is too kind, but it was not of my doing. His lordship insisted...' The valet's tone expressed his disapproval of the whole affair.

'Well, then, we must all obey his lordship's express wish, must we not?' Georgiana hid a smile. She had routed Scroggins without difficulty, and he knew it.

'Look Betsy! Do you see the men in sabots? Those are the clog-like shoes they wear upon their feet...' Georgiana chattered artlessly as they drove along the dockside, drawing a shy response from Betsy until the girl was more herself again.

It was but a short journey to the hotel, but she was dismayed to find that they were to stay at Dessein's. She might have known, she thought bitterly. It was the only suitable destination for an English gentleman.

Anxiously she scanned the crowds in the foyer, dreading to see either Harry or Richard. Yet surely the Viscount would not indulge in a public altercation? She shuddered. It was more than likely that they would encounter the two fugitives this very day. If only she could buy time to warn Harry of the Viscount's presence in the town.

Lyndhurst wasted no time. Within minutes of their arrival he questioned Monsieur Quillac, the proprietor.

It was with an overwhelming sense of relief that Georgiana heard the Frenchman disclaim all knowledge of Messieurs Thorpe and Westleigh. Now, with any luck at all, Harry might see the coat-of-arms upon the Viscount's carriage and realise the danger.

Her hopes were dashed when Lyndhurst asked for stabling for the night. His coach would soon be out of sight.

She was inspecting her meagre wardrobe when Scroggins brought her a message.

'His lordship wishes you to join him in the parlour, madam.' The valet avoided her eye and looked at his niece. 'With your permission I will have a word with Betsy.'

'Please do! Did I mention how pleased I am with her?' Georgiana gave him a brilliant smile. Then, having forestalled any criticism of his niece, she went to meet the Viscount.

He was standing by the fireplace when she entered the room, a deep frown creasing his brow.

'You will please to tell me of your arrangements with your brother,' he said without preamble. 'I had hoped to find him here with Richard, but there is no word of them. Now, it would appear, we must search the town.'

'Dessein's is expensive,' Georgiana murmured in a low voice. 'You forget, my lord, they cannot have much money to hand after their flight.'

'I don't doubt it,' came the dry reply. 'They have scattered gold like chaff in their haste to get away...but you do not answer my question.'

At a loss for words, Georgiana turned away from his penetrating gaze.

'They would not stay here,' she muttered. 'Is this not the first place that anyone would search for them?'

'It is. But do not prevaricate, Miss Westleigh. They are not here, but you must know how to find your brother.'

'You are mistaken. Our arrangement was that he should find me.'

'Then he will come here?' The keen blue eyes searched her face.

'Possibly...'

'I see. You were to stay here in any case. You must have hoped for a handsome return on the sale of your possessions...'

Her green eyes blazed at him. 'There is no need to remind me that I am beholden to you. I will leave whenever you wish.'

She heard a contemptuous laugh.

'I think you are well aware that I shall not do

that. You are the only card I hold, but to be the lure will be no new experience for you, I imagine.'

'You may imagine what you will. Whatever it is, it gave you no right to…to…'

'Assault your person? Come now, don't play the innocent with me. A single kiss, Miss West-leigh, which, I may add, you returned with interest? It was the impulse of a moment, and doubtless meant as little to you as it did to me.'

Georgiana could have struck him.

'Meaningless, I agree,' she said in icy tones. 'How could it be otherwise? My opinion of you is now quite as low as yours of me. Strangely, I expected better of you. I shall not make that mistake again.'

His laugh was derisive.

'Outraged virtue…coming from you? Will you deny that your charms played their part in persuading your brother's victims to agree to his schemes?'

'I do deny it,' Georgiana cried hotly. 'Though I don't expect you to believe me.' Her hands were shaking with rage, and she thrust them out of sight within the folds of her gown.

'Why should I?' came the cynical reply. 'Doubtless you are proud of your ability to deceive.'

'You may think what you wish,' she ground out. 'You know nothing of the matter, yet you are prepared to judge.'

'If necessary I shall be judge, jury and executioner.' The blue eyes were chips of ice, and his expression was forbidding. 'Now get your cloak. We shall take a stroll about the town.'

'I do not care to accompany you.' Georgiana was in no doubt as to his purpose. He was hoping to come upon the fugitives unawares.

'Yet you will do so. I don't intend to leave you here to warn your brother should he appear in my absence.'

Further argument would be fruitless, she knew. She fetched her cloak, and in silence, allowed her companion to lead her into the street. The storm of the previous night had cleared the air, and the first rays of the sun, breaking through cloud, brought the promise of a fine June day.

Georgiana's heart lifted, in spite of her fear that they might come upon Harry and Richard in the course of their promenade about the narrow streets. She would keep her wits about her. If the worst came to the worst, she could distract Lyndhurst's attention by pretending to faint. There was always the possibility that he would not be taken in. She must think of another stratagem.

She put up her hand to clutch at her bonnet as the wind threatened to tear it from her head. The gusts were fierce, and they stirred up swirling clouds of dust which settled upon bonnet, cloak, and even left a powdery grey deposit on the skirt of her primrose muslin gown. The gritty particles found their way beneath her eyelids, and she averted her head. The stinging sensation was unbearable. With watering eyes she felt in her reticule for a handkerchief.

'Don't rub at them. You will make matters worse.' Lyndhurst took the scrap of lace-edged cambric from her. 'Come here.' He drew her into the shelter of a doorway. 'Now let me see.'

His fingers were surprisingly gentle as he lifted her upper lids. 'Now keep quite still,' he ordered. 'Just moisten your handkerchief and give it to me. You have a cinder or something of the kind in your left eye.'

Georgiana did as she was bidden. His face was very close to hers, but she was in too much pain to refuse his help. His fingers were cool and infinitely careful as he held her face steady, prising open the eyelid again.

'Don't blink. There…I have it now. Is that better?'

Georgiana mopped her streaming eyes and blew her nose.

'It's a great relief,' she said with feeling. 'It felt like a mountain.'

'Just a speck of grit.'

There was an odd note in his voice and she looked up quickly to find that he was eyeing her with concern.

'I must look a perfect fright,' she muttered, more to herself than to him.

'Not at all! Apart from two reddened eyes and a swollen nose, you are your usual ravishing self.'

'Thank you!' She threw him an angry look, only to find that he was laughing. 'I fail to see what you find so amusing, my lord.'

'Just your injured dignity, my dear. When your feathers are ruffled you are quite enchanting.' He drew her arm through his. 'Shall we continue our walk?'

Georgiana was tempted to pull away from him, but he sensed her intention and laid his free hand on the arm resting within his own.

'I think not,' he said in a soft voice. 'Even your dignity would not withstand an unseemly fracas in the street.'

She had no alternative but to continue to pace

beside him, aware that he was matching his long stride to her shorter steps.

'Well, this is all very pleasant, Miss Westleigh. Sunshine, the sea air, and a beautiful woman on my arm. What more could a man ask? Such a pity that we are here on an unpleasant errand.'

A solitary figure strolling along the quayside towards them drew her attention. At first sight his dress was unremarkable. There was nothing in it to cause the passer-by to ignore his height, his handsome countenance, and the perfection of his bow as he drew abreast of them.

'Who is that man?' she asked in a low voice.

'That is George Brummell, Miss Westleigh. You are not acquainted with him?' The Viscount did not return the bow.

'I have not seen him before. He is unlike I imagined.'

The Viscount's laugh was unpleasant.

'You should study the set of his coat, the cut of his pantaloons, and the arrangement of his cravat. He is said to have employed two firms to make his gloves…one for the fingers and the other for the thumbs.' His tone left her in no doubt as to his opinion of a fellow who devoted his life to such trivialities.

'Poor soul!' Georgiana looked back at the lonely walker. 'It is sad indeed that after the life he has led he should be forced to flee to escape his creditors. I hear that he was a kindly man, thoughtful for his friends.'

'Save your pity for those he duped,' Lyndhurst said sharply. 'I suppose I should not be surprised at your fellow-feeling for him.'

'I'm sure he meant well.' Georgiana's temper flared. 'Many business ventures go awry.'

'They do. But a clear intention to steal a man's patrimony with the promise in return of an income for life cannot be excused.' His lips curled in contempt as he looked at her. 'You and your kind are leeches upon the gullible.'

He was baiting her again, and her temper rose further. 'That is of your own doing,' she told him. 'This "errand", as you term it, need not continue.'

'I think it must,' he said mildly. 'What would you have me do? Shall I turn tail and return to England, leaving you here to enjoy your ill-gotten gains?'

'We have no gains, and well you know it. We are stripped of everything. Is not that enough for you?'

'Not quite.'

'So you will have your pound of flesh?' It was

meant as an insult, but to her astonishment he threw back his head and roared with laughter.

'I see that I am discovered. Miss Westleigh, you underestimate yourself. I am persuaded that you weigh far more than a mere pound.'

His effrontery took Georgiana's breath away.

'Oh!' she cried. 'I might have known that you would seize every opportunity to insult me. I was quoting Shakespeare, sir. Have you not read *The Merchant of Venice?* The villain Shylock is not swayed by mercy or love of his fellow creatures. He means to destroy his victim utterly.'

'I could be persuaded to love my fellow creatures…or at least one of them.' Lyndhurst's eyes held a mischievous glint. 'And after all, Miss Westleigh, you indicated only an hour ago that my lust for you is obvious.'

'I said no such thing.' Georgiana coloured to the ears. 'It was just that…well, you had no right to…to…'

'To kiss you? But, my dear, you kissed me back. It was quite an experience. Your demure appearance gives no hint of the fires which burn below. Yet I should, perhaps, have guessed. Those flashing jade-green eyes, and that fiery mane of yours… Ah, yes, I should have guessed.'

Georgiana was speechless with embarrassment. She had been a fool to think herself safe with this man. His brother did not know him. This was no cold fish, but a passionate and demanding creature who would take his pleasure with a woman as it suited him.

She felt a twinge of fear, but whether it was fear of him, or of her own undoubted response to his caresses, she could not decide. Either way, she must escape from him at the earliest opportunity, or she would not answer for the consequences.

With an effort she forced herself to speak.

'You are mistaken in me, my lord, and your remarks are insulting. I have no…no experience of an embrace.' She could not look at him, but even as she spoke she knew that her words were a mistake.

Lyndhurst checked his stride and turned to face her. 'Then you must allow me to compliment you. Given an expert teacher an asset such as yours is beyond price.'

Georgiana's eyes filled with tears. It was a cruel gibe. Was she now to be despised for her natural feelings as a woman?

Blindly she threw out a hand as if to ward off a blow, and found it held in a firm clasp.

'We had best go back.' Lyndhurst's voice was raw with an emotion she could not place. He strode along, almost dragging her back to the inn, until she found herself running to keep up with him.

Ignoring the curious faces in the foyer, he hurried her up to their parlour and thrust her into a chair. Weariness overcame her as she looked at the clenched jaw and the grim line of his mouth. What had she done now to displease him?

'My lord, I am tired,' she whispered. 'I should like to go to my room.'

'Presently. But first I have something to say to you.'

Whatever it was, the Viscount seemed to be in some difficulty as to how to begin. He paced the room for several minutes. Then he thrust a clenched fist into the palm of his other hand and swung round to face her.

'You have succeeded in making me ashamed of myself, Miss Westleigh.' His smile was agonised. 'My behaviour was insufferable.'

Georgiana did not reply. She could not gainsay his words, and yet there seemed little point in agreeing with him.

'I cannot think why… Well, yes, I can… There

is nothing quite so ridiculous as a man at war with himself.'

Puzzled, she looked up at him then. The thick brown crop of hair was tousled, and a lock or two had fallen on to his brow. It gave him the look of a penitent schoolboy.

In spite of herself she smiled at the thought. Then he was on his knees beside her chair.

'Sometimes I forget how young you are,' he murmured. 'You had no need to tell me of your inexperience. An older woman would have made sport of me long since. But you…you do not guess?' Another long look and then he rose to his feet.

'Forgive me,' he said abruptly. 'I have no right to burden you with this nonsense. Suffice it to say that I should be horsewhipped for my incivility.'

Georgiana shot him a slanting glance from under her lashes.

'What a passion you have for horsewhips, sir! You have the instrument with you? I wonder if anyone would dare to use it?'

He gave her an uncertain look, and then an unwilling smile.

'You are generous to make a joke of this matter, Miss Westleigh. It is more than I deserve.'

'You are very hard on yourself, my lord. If we

all got what we deserved the world would be a strange place.' She smiled back at him. 'Now, if you will excuse me…?'

As she rose he moved towards her. For a second she thought that he would take her in his arms, but he checked himself, and bowed. Then he raised her hand to his lips.

'You are a pearl among women,' he said thickly. Then he was gone, leaving her with only the memory of his warm mouth against her flesh. Raising the hand to her cheek, she walked slowly into her bedroom.

She would never understand this stranger who had come without warning into her life.

He could be detestable. She was not surprised that his brother feared the flaying power of his tongue. From her own experience she knew that Lyndhurst could be deeply wounding when he suspected low moral standards in others. Her cheeks grew hot as she thought of his words to her.

Yet could she blame him? On the evidence she had supported her own brother without question, and still planned to do so. And, in spite of the Viscount's belief that she was little better than a criminal, he had been quick to apologise when he'd seen her distress.

He was the oddest mixture of contradictions. What on earth could he have meant by speaking of a man at war with himself? He found her physically attractive. He had made that only too clear. Was he fighting his own desire for a woman who had entrusted herself to his care?

Involuntarily Georgiana shook her head. His lordship, blessed as he was with title, wealth, and an imposing appearance, might have any number of women. He would think it beneath his dignity to force himself upon an unwilling partner.

Then what? Had he meant that he was beginning to change his mind as to the punishment he intended for Harry and his own brother? She doubted it. His face closed whenever he spoke of the two fugitives, and his words were openly contemptuous.

She worried at the question again. Why should a man be at war with himself? He seemed to think that she ought to know. It could not be that he was softening towards her...

Georgiana's eyes grew dreamy. It was not that she cared, of course, but it would be pleasant to think that he no longer regarded her as a liar and a cheat. He had looked so different when he had begged her pardon for his cruel words. The grim expression had given way to a look which was almost vulnerable… She had longed to throw her arms about him and hold him close as she forgave him.

She collected her wandering thoughts with a start. Her imagination was running wild. It was just that when he was close she felt an overwhelming urge to touch him, to stroke his cheek, to caress that unruly crop of thick brown hair, and to see the slow smile which began at the back of his eyes and grew until it seemed to envelop her in pleasure.

Great heavens! She was behaving like some foolish miss swept off her feet by a first kiss. The touch of his lips on her mouth had shaken her, but it had been meaningless. He had said so himself, but for her own part she found it hard to believe. Would she ever feel that surging, dizzying rapture with another man?

A growing sense of depression seized her. What a mess she and Harry had made of their lives. It was useless to dwell on what might have been, or even to hope that Lyndhurst thought better of her. When Harry found her she would flee with him, and all the Viscount's suspicion of her motives would be confirmed. Nothing she said or did would persuade him to trust her again, but it did not matter. She would have vanished from his life.

She felt so low in spirits that it was a relief

when Scroggins appeared with a message from Lyndhurst. His lordship had been called away, and she must dine alone.

A prickle of apprehension ran down Georgiana's spine. Had he received news of Richard and Harry?

'Is…is it something important?' she faltered. It went against the grain to question Scroggins, but she must know.

The man looked at her in silence, and she sensed his hostility.

'I asked you a question,' she said coldly.

'His lordship does not confide in me, madam. I fear I cannot help you.'

'Cannot or will not?' With a gesture of impatience she brushed past him. Lyndhurst might not yet have left for his appointment. She hurried along the corridor to the door of the adjoining room, but her quick knock brought no response.

'You will excuse me for addressing you, ma'am, but I believe that Viscount Lyndhurst is at present in the foyer.'

Georgiana looked round in surprise. The speaker was a tall, thin man dressed in the height of fashion. A clever, somewhat narrow face was crowned with a thatch of greying hair, but it was his eyes which held her attention. Their silver gaze was almost hypnotic. Not a man one would care to claim as an enemy, she thought at once.

With an effort she looked away and nodded her thanks. Then she sped down the stairs and into the crowded foyer.

From her vantage point on the bottom stair she scanned the bustling throng. As he was taller and broader than the men about him, she saw the Viscount at once, but to her dismay he was strolling towards the doorway which led into the street.

With muttered apologies for her haste she thrust her way towards him, attracting curious glances from those close to her.

'My lord?'

He turned at once and reached her side in a couple of swift strides.

'Is something wrong?'

'No, no…at least…when Scroggins gave me your message I thought you might have heard…'

A faint look of annoyance crossed his face. Her breathless words had carried to other ears, and for the moment they were the centre of attention.

Lyndhurst took her elbow and drew her into the relative privacy of a recess.

'You will not wish to conduct our conversation in public, I imagine, Miss Westleigh.' His eyes swept over her, and Georgiana was aware that she must present a dishevelled appearance, without bonnet or cloak, and still panting from her efforts to push through the crowd. She brushed such considerations aside.

'You would tell me, wouldn't you?' she pleaded.

'I have heard nothing.' His voice was cold initially. Then it softened in the face of her evident anxiety. 'I received an invitation to dine at the British Consulate. I take it I have your permission to see my friends there?'

Georgiana hung her head and her cheeks grew rosy.

'I'm sorry,' she whispered. 'I would not have you think that I spy upon your every movement.'

'That would be foolish,' he agreed. 'Now may I suggest that you return to your room? You are looking fagged and much in need of rest...' He took her arm in a firm grip and steered her back through the crowds towards the staircase.

As he raised his hat to leave her she made a final plea.

'My lord, should you hear of Harry and Richard, will you give me your word that you will do nothing until you have spoken to me?'

Lyndhurst gave her a long, considering look. Then his lips twitched. 'What will you do, my pretty tigress, to save them from my wrath?'

She could not answer him.

'Think about it,' he advised. 'Meantime, you may have my word that when they are discovered you shall be the first to hear of it.'

It was scant comfort, but at least she had his promise. As she started up the stairs she had a curious sensation of being watched. She turned, to find that the man who had spoken to her earlier was standing in the shadow of the stairwell.

A little shiver ran down her spine. Somehow his presence in Calais troubled her. How had the stranger known that she was seeking Lyndhurst? He must have asked the landlord for the direction of the Viscount's room, yet he had not claimed acquaintance of his lordship.

It was a mystery. The man was no dun, she was sure of it. He looked every inch the gentleman. Could he be one of Harry's victims? It seemed unlikely. The stranger had a predatory look about him. At a guess he would be the attacker rather than the victim.

She could feel his eyes following her as she climbed the stairs, and suddenly she longed for the comfort of Lyndhurst's presence. In his company she always felt so safe.

She should have told him at once about the stranger, but there had been no time. In any case he most probably would have laughed her to scorn for allowing her imagination to run wild. The man's rooms could well be on the same corridor, and he might have seen Lyndhurst leaving his room. What more natural that he should ask the name of a fellow Englishman? That the stranger was English she had no doubt.

Having reasoned away her fears, she entered her private parlour to find that a light nuncheon had been laid for her. Still lost in thought, she took a little of the cold meats and salad, but it tasted like ashes in her mouth. She must be over-tired. Lyndhurst himself had said that she was looking fagged.

She was amused in spite of her indignation at the frank remark. One might expect nothing but the plain, unvarnished truth from his lordship.

She pushed her plate away and wandered into her bedroom. There she looked thoughtfully at her reflection in the glass. Lyndhurst had not exaggerated. Her eyes looked larger than ever in the piquant face, but dark circles had appeared beneath them.

She felt unutterably weary, and without troubling to remove her gown she lay upon the bed. She should have been making plans, but how could she plan when she had no word of Harry? Lyndhurst would keep her close, and how was she to escape his vigilance?

It was strange that the thought of leaving him gave her no pleasure. After all, she had accomplished the first part of her mission. She was here in Calais, but what was she to do now?

She closed her eyes, allowing her thoughts to drift. It was all too much effort, and she was very tired. If she rested now her mind would clear.

It was early evening when she awoke, and the bustle in the street outside had lessened. She struggled to sit up as the door opened and Betsy arrived with a pile of clothing over her arm.

'I've washed your underclothing, miss, and pressed your gowns.' Betsy's cheeks were flushed and her eyes were sparkling. She had evidently recovered her spirits.

Georgiana smiled her thanks. 'Will you ring for hot water, Betsy? I feel so grubby. Then you may help me dress.'

With the girl's help she made her toilette, shaking her head as she looked at her meagre wardrobe. She had packed so quickly in her haste to get away. Had she really only brought three thin gowns? She shrugged. The leaf-green muslin would have to do again. It did not matter. She would be alone for the rest of what promised to be a long and dreary evening.

Never had the time seemed to go so slowly. Georgiana attempted to do justice to the excellent meal which was served at nine, but she could do no more than toy with the food.

Then she picked up a copy of *La Belle Assemblée*, thoughtfully provided by the landlord, but the fashions did not interest her. Half-heartedly she made an effort to translate the text. If she and Harry were to live in France she must improve her halting, schoolgirl efforts to understand the language.

It was in vain. She could not concentrate, and the room seemed so stuffy. Did the French never open their windows?

She remembered the balcony outside her bedroom window. There, at least, she could enjoy the fresh air. She returned to her room and flung the windows wide. It was a heavenly night, with a crescent moon and a scattering of stars in the summer sky.

Georgiana dragged a chair outside and sat lost in thought for what seemed like hours. What was to become of Harry and herself? She could find no comforting solution to her problems, but she must not think of the long, lonely years ahead. She had not thought to end her days as a spinster, but she and Harry were inextricably tied together. She could never leave him.

The air was growing chill. She left her seat on the balcony, leaving the window open. She was about to ring for Betsy when a sudden noise alerted her.

'Don't touch the bell!' Harry was smiling as he stepped through the open windows. 'How are you, my dear?'

Chapter Five

'Harry!' With a muffled sob Georgiana stumbled towards him, holding out both her hands. 'I've been so worried about you.'

Harry gave her a brotherly hug, and tweaked at a copper curl. 'No need to get into a taking, Georgie. All is well.'

'All is far from well,' she cried in exasperation. 'You do not realise…Lyndhurst is here in Calais. He is searching for Richard, and for you too.'

'I had heard, but I'm not afraid of him.' His words lacked conviction, and his bravado cost him an effort, but he forced another smile. 'What can he do? He could scarce carry us bodily back to England.'

'Don't be foolish! At the very least he has promised you a horsewhipping.'

Harry's smile vanished and he paled. 'Why did you lead him to us?' he demanded. 'And what are you doing in his company anyway?'

'I had no choice. Without him I could not have come here.' She gave him the gist of her story in pithy terms and he had the grace to look ashamed.

'I had no idea, else I would not have left you.'

'That is the trouble, Harry. To say that you had no idea is not an excuse worth considering. Is it not time you showed some common sense?'

'Don't preach!' His face grew sullen. 'Your sound like Lyndhurst himself.'

Georgiana bit back the words which were upon her tongue. There was no point in quarrelling with him.

'How did you find me?' she asked.

'I have my sources.' The injured expression still lingered on his face. It had come as a shock to be criticised so sharply by his adoring elder sister.

Georgiana ignored it. She felt too irritated to attempt to wheedle him into a better humour. Instead she changed the subject.

'Lyndhurst is not our only worry,' she said quietly. 'There is another Englishman in the hotel. I fear he has been watching me.'

To her surprise he smiled. 'Tall and thin, with greying hair?'

'Why, yes! Do you know him?'

'I told you I had sources.' He had not given her a direct answer, and his evasive reply did nothing to reassure her.

'Did you meet him in London? What is his name?' Every instinct warned her against the mysterious stranger. She sensed that he was a dangerous man. If he was an example of Harry's latest friends her brother's future, and her own, promised to be disastrous.

Harry made a gesture of impatience. 'Must you quiz me now? Lyndhurst may be back at any moment.' He glanced towards the door. In spite of his protestations she guessed that he would not relish a meeting with the Viscount.

'His lordship dines at the British Consulate,' she said in a cool tone. 'We shall be undisturbed. Now, Harry, what are we to do?'

'We must get away, of course. Calais is too close to England, and too dangerous. In Paris we might lose ourselves among the crowd.'

'Lyndhurst will follow you,' Georgiana observed quietly.

'Well, then Rome…or Vienna… It cannot signify. In a large city we may hide…'

'A hole-and-corner existence? How are we to live?'

An angry retort rose to his lips, but a glance at her face stemmed the bitter words before he spoke.

'You are tired, dear love.' Privately he was appalled to see the dark circles beneath her eyes and her look of strain. He sat down suddenly and buried his face in his hands.

'Oh, Georgie, I am so sorry,' he said in a muffled voice. 'I did not intend to drag you down with me.'

She laid a hand upon the flaming curls so like her own. 'I fear we shall have to dye our hair, my dear. This colour is like a beacon in a crowd.'

Harry looked up then, to see a faint smile on her face. She bent and kissed his brow.

'When do we leave?' she asked.

He was on his feet at once, his eyes alight with eagerness.

'Tomorrow night,' he announced. 'There is no time to lose, and Richard is in a state because of Lyndhurst.'

'I can imagine.' Georgiana's voice was dry, but Harry did not notice.

'I believe old sourpuss keeps you close,' he continued. 'You must plead illness or some such thing. Then you may keep to your room, although we cannot travel in daylight. I'll come for you about this time tomorrow.'

Strangely, the thought gave her no pleasure.

'Is there no other way?' she asked without much hope. 'The Viscount must have some family feeling. If Richard were to see him and explain...'

Harry stared at her. 'Have you run quite mad? You told me yourself that he thinks only in terms of a horsewhipping. Dear God!' He threw his eyes to heaven. 'To expect a hearing from that prune-faced...'

Georgiana lost her temper then, and her face grew white with anger. 'Must you be so childish?' she demanded coldly. 'Name-calling? You might be five years old...'

'Never say that he has brought you to his way of thinking. That stiff-necked model of rectitude... He is filled with righteous anger, I suppose?'

'And has he not cause? Harry, he mentioned fraud.'

'Stuff! What does he know of our affairs?'

'Quite a lot, it would appear. Is it true that you took large sums of money on a promise of annual payments?'

'It is accepted practice.' His face was sullen. 'Brummell and his friends had a similar scheme…'

'And Brummell is now in a similar position to you. We saw him today. He is disgraced. No one will acknowledge him.'

'By that I imagine you mean that Lyndhurst found it necessary to cut him dead in case a simple greeting might pollute his noble character?'

Georgiana ignored the taunt. 'Brummell can never return to England, Harry. He is forced into exile, as we are ourselves. Oh, my dear, how could you have been so foolish? And to cheat people of their savings…'

A dark flush stained Harry's cheeks. He was unused to such plain speaking from his sister. In her eyes he could do non wrong—or at least he'd thought so until now…

'How do you think we lived?' he said defensively. 'We had the house in London. You enjoyed the balls and entertainments…to say nothing of your dressmakers' bills.'

'I had rather have gone in rags.' She turned away from him. 'You deceived me, Harry. Did you not say that you won thousands at the tables?'

He was saved from the need to reply by a tap at the door. Georgiana looked at him in dismay.

'Quickly!' She pushed him towards the window. 'Hide behind the curtains. I'll send Betsy away.'

But her late-night visitor was the Viscount. He stood in the doorway smiling down at her.

'Forgive me for troubling you at this hour, but I saw your light from the street. I thought you might sleep better for the knowledge that our erring relatives have been seen in Calais…'

Georgiana was silent.

'My dear, you are trembling. Am I such an ogre, then?'

Her eyes were huge with fright as she looked into his own, and a troubled frown creased his brow.

'I see that I am,' he said abruptly. 'Believe me, Miss Westleigh, I wish only what is best for both our families. May I ask you to give me your trust?'

Speechless, she nodded her assent.

'Then I will wish you a good night's rest.' He looked beyond her to the open window, and as if in a trance she followed his gaze. Was it a breeze that stirred the curtains?

'You should close your window,' he murmured. 'The air is chill.'

As Georgiana closed her door her brother appeared from behind the curtains.

'I hope you don't believe a word of that charming speech,' he snapped. 'Trust him to do what is best indeed!'

'I do trust him.' Georgiana lost the last traces of her self-control. 'He, at least, is a man who keeps his word.'

Harry went very white about the lips. The blow had struck home.

'No, please!' She put a weary hand to her head. 'I did not mean that to sound so harsh, but, you see, I cannot complain of the Viscount's care for me.'

'With at least one purpose in mind…that of finding us. I wonder if he had another…?'

He was unprepared for her stinging slap across his cheek.

'How dare you?' she cried furiously. 'You left me to fend for myself.'

Harry had the grace to look ashamed. 'I was angry, and I spoke in haste,' he muttered. 'Of course I did not think that you…that he… That dry stick! I doubt if he's ever looked at a woman in his life. I beg your pardon. Georgie, dear, I'm not myself tonight.'

When she did not reply he stole a glance at her, but she averted her head.

'I didn't mean that he wouldn't be tempted by you,' he offered. 'That would be an insult…but…'

'Harry, you are making matters worse.' Georgiana was torn between laughter and tears. 'You had best go before you get deeper into the mire…'

'Then I am forgiven?' He threw an arm about her shoulders. 'We must stick together, love. You are all I have in the world.'

'I know.' She put up her face for a kiss, though her heart was filled with despair. 'Don't worry… I shall be ready when you come.'

She heard a faint scuffle as he lowered himself by the creeper outside her window, and then a low thud as he dropped into the street. With a sigh she closed the curtains, and began to struggle out of her gown. It was much too late to ring for Betsy. The girl would be long asleep, and she hadn't the heart to wake her. In any case, she needed time to collect her thoughts.

Since his unreserved apology earlier in the day, Lyndhurst's manner towards her had been different. It was softer, gentler and more tolerant. Oh, if only she'd had more time. She might have persuaded him to forgive Harry and his brother.

It was too late now. The die was cast. She would have but one more day in his company, and then he would vanish from her life forever.

She slipped into her bedrobe and lay down, but sleep would not come. To her horror she found that slow tears were beginning to trickle down her cheeks. What a fool she was! She should have been elated. Had she not achieved her object in coming to France? She had found Harry, and now they were to start their new life together, safe in some European city.

The prospect had no power to lift her spirits. She could think only of the long years ahead, living from hand to mouth, and relying only on Harry's ability to provide for her. Would he resort to underhand dealings again?

Sadly, she realised that she could no longer trust him. Her idol had feet of clay, and she herself was partly to blame for his cavalier attitude to life. Her unquestioning support had done him no service. Her affection had blinded her to his faults, but now she saw them only too clearly.

She would have to think for both of them, and keep him on a steady path if possible. It would be a daunting task, and the thought of it was too much for her tired mind.

Weariness overcame her and she drifted into sleep at last with the memory of a pair of clear blue eyes gazing into her own.

* * *

She awoke to find that sunlight was filing the room. In the few seconds before full consciousness returned she stretched luxuriously, fully prepared to enjoy the pleasure of a perfect summer day. Then she remembered, and her spirits sank. Today was to end in a parting which she could only dread. But why?

Swiftly, she tried to control her unguarded thoughts, but it was no longer possible to deceive herself. She loved Lyndhurst with a passion which shook her to the core of her being.

Since Harry's disgrace she had not thought it possible to feel more wretched, but now she could have screamed in agony. Her happiness was to be thrown away...for what? Why had she ever met that cool, imperious figure who could raise her to the heights of rapture with a kiss, or crush her with a frown? She must stop thinking about him, and above all she must not betray herself. He would only despise her the more.

She should have insisted on leaving with Harry on the previous evening, she thought to herself. That way she might have escaped the torture which awaited her in the coming hours. It seemed that she was to be spared none of it.

Betsy confirmed her fears.

'I was to tell his lordship when you wakened, miss.' Betsy had drawn the curtains and was laying out Georgiana's clothes. 'He's waiting for you in the parlour. Must I go now?'

Georgiana drew a deep breath. 'I shall not be long, though he should not wait to break his fast. I find that I am not hungry.'

Her eye fell on the white sprigged muslin hanging by the door. It had always been a favourite gown, but now it looked much too festive for her sombre mood.

'I can't wear that,' she muttered.

Betsy's face fell. 'Miss, it's all you've got. You lay on your bed in one of your gowns, and the other needs a wash.'

'Very well. Come back when you've seen his lordship.'

Quickly she bathed her face and hands, hoping that the warm, scented water would restore her spirits. She did feel a little better as she dressed, but how was she to get through the day without betraying herself? She might hide her emotions with some success, but she feared Lyndhurst's piercing gaze. Surely he would suspect that something was amiss?

When she entered the parlour he was standing

by the window, but he turned at once. His expression was a tribute to her beauty. He walked towards her and took her hand.

'I did not obey your orders,' he said lightly. 'There is something too depressing about dining alone.'

With grave courtesy he seated her at the table, and signalled to the waiting servants.

Georgiana was tempted to refuse the shirred eggs, the pink, succulent slices of ham, and the kidneys in Madeira, but she dared not. He gave her a long, considering glance.

'There is still room for improvement,' he said at last. 'Miss Westleigh, I propose to take you for a drive this morning. The day is fine, the wind has dropped, and you look much in need of a change.'

His words were kindly meant. How could he know that he was turning the knife in the wound? Had she not hoped that he would have other plans, which would take him out of her sight? Her heart gave her the lie. Every moment together would be cherished and remembered for the rest of her life. Still she demurred.

'You do not wish to make further enquiries…about Richard and Harry?'

He gave her a heart-stopping smile.

'My dear Miss Westleigh, our youthful relatives are beginning to bore me. Let us forget them for today. Enough is enough, you will agree?'

'But…'

'No buts… We have concerned ourselves with them for too long. Is it too much to ask that we allow a few hours for ourselves?'

'It is kind in you, but…' She hesitated, and then went on in a rush. 'My lord, you must not feel obliged… I am quite well. It is just that I have not…'

'You have not been sleeping easily? That, my dear, is plain to see. But you promised to trust me, did you not? Will you leave matters in my hands?'

Georgiana could not look at him. His voice was so gentle that she felt like bursting into tears. If only she might have persuaded Harry and Richard to speak to him. They would feel the rough edge of his tongue, and it would be an unpleasant interview, but Lyndhurst, she was now convinced, would find a way out of their difficulties.

When she did not reply he reached across the table and took her hand in his. 'Georgiana, look at me! Do you still believe that I wish you harm?'

It was the first time he had used her given name, and she felt a little glow of happiness. Obediently, she raised her eyes to his and shook her head. That question, at least, she could answer truthfully.

She left her hand in his, longing to curl her fingers about his own. Did he guess at the inner turmoil which swept her every time he touched her? She prayed that he did not. At that moment she could have thrown herself into his arms and told him everything.

But that would mean betraying Harry, and she had given her word to leave with him that very night. She grew cold at the thought of the deception which she planned to carry out against the man she loved so much.

She had been such a fool. She should have pleaded sickness…a headache…anything to avoid the sweet torture of these last few hours with him. It was not too late to make some excuse to return to her room.

She wavered, but as the blue eyes locked with her own she was lost. Just a few more hours of happiness? It was little enough to carry with her in memory through the years ahead.

She was surprised to see a high-perch phaeton at the door, but the Viscount handed her up without comment and took the reins himself.

'You are warm enough?' He tucked a rug about

her knees. Then he guided the team through the narrow streets of Calais towards the open countryside.

Wretched though she was at the thought of her deception, Georgiana felt her spirits lift as they bowled along. The sky was a cloudless blue, and she could smell the salt sea air. High above the wheeling gulls called harshly as they swooped towards the returning fishing boats, and she smiled at their effortless skill.

'I cannot promise you much in the way of scenery.' Lyndhurst had turned inland. 'This part of France is somewhat bleak and featureless, but further south... Ah, there you may see this country at its best.'

'It does not matter.' Georgiana looked up at him shyly. 'I am happy to be here.'

He stopped the carriage at once. A strong hand rested on her shoulder and he turned her round towards him.

'Are you?' The steady eyes searched her face. 'Then so am I.' A lean finger reached up to smooth away a straying copper curl. 'My dear, I have given you no cause to think of me with kindness, but I could wish...'

'Please don't,' she cried in panic. 'Do not say more.'

'Why not?' He had drawn her close, and his lips were nuzzling her cheek. 'Georgiana, my darling, have you not guessed how much I care for you? God knows I have been behaving like a lunatic these last few days, blaming myself for ending my own hopes with my cruelty towards you, and yet hoping that you might see...'

'I did not suspect, else I should not have come,' she told him in a muffled voice. 'Please take me back to Calais.'

This was worse than she could possibly have imagined. To be offered the promise of happiness beyond her dreams only to reject it? The anguish was unbearable.

'My dearest!' He was dropping light kisses upon her brow, her eyelids and her cheeks. 'Can I have been mistaken? Will you deny that when we kissed you felt as I did? There is a bond between us which cannot be broken.'

'You told me that the kiss was meaningless.' It cost her an effort to speak with a lightness she was far from feeling.

'I was lying, as much to myself as to you. I fought my love with all my mind but my heart will be still no longer. My darling Georgiana, will you be my wife?'

'I cannot.' She turned her head too quickly and he claimed her lips. Again she was borne on a dizzying tide of rapture as the warm mouth rested on her own. A warm, unfamiliar sensation swept through her body, urging her to a greater closeness. Of her own volition she threw her arms about his neck, arching her back as he bent over her. By the time he released her she was breathless.

'You are a witch.' He looked down tenderly at her rosy face. 'Will you tease me further by saying that you do not care for me?'

Wildly, Georgiana cast about for some answer that would satisfy him.

'You must give me time,' she pleaded in a low voice.

Even to her own ears the words sounded feeble, but she could think of nothing else to say. It was too late to deny her love. Her own response to him would have given her the lie.

'There is much to consider,' she murmured at last, aware of his sharp eyes on her face.

'Still thinking of your precious Harry?' His tone was sardonic, but she sensed the hurt behind his words.

'I must think of him,' she replied. 'I cannot abandon him. He has no one else who cares…'

'I shall not harm him. That, at least, you must believe.'

'I do.' The temptation to confide in him was overwhelming, but she resisted it. 'I asked only for a little time...'

'As you wish.' He gave her a faint smile, and picked up the reins once more. He was silent for the rest of their drive, and Georgiana was left to the scant comfort of her own thoughts.

She had made up her mind before the returned to the inn. When Harry returned that night she would make him see reason. If she could but convince him that he might trust Lyndhurst he would give up his ridiculous plans to scratch a living in some foreign city.

And Richard would follow his lead. Even on brief acquaintance with the Viscount's brother she had learned that Harry was the stronger character of the two. Though that was not saying much, she would admit.

Her face cleared. The very fact of coming to a decision had lightened her heart. She had no idea how Lyndhurst meant to handle the situation, and he had given her no indication, but she was sure that he would find a solution.

She stole a glance at his clean-cut profile. As if

sensing her regard he looked down at her and the blue eyes held hers captive.

'As I expected, our drive has done you good,' he said gently. 'The shadows have disappeared, my dear. I intend to see that they never return. It breaks my heart to see you in distress.'

'You are very good.' She rested a gloved hand upon his arm. 'You must not believe that I am behaving like some schoolroom miss, my lord. I did not intend to sound so...so formal.'

He swung down and reached up his arms for her. 'Your formality slipped a little, I believe.' He laughed as she began to blush. 'At least you were kind enough not to tell me that my proposal was so sudden, or that you thanked me for the honour I had done you. Words such as those would have ended my hopes at once.'

Georgiana gave him a sweet smile. Her flushed cheeks and her sparkling eyes betrayed her love as clearly as if she had shouted it aloud. Eagerly he moved towards her, but she shook her head and hurried into the hotel. She must speak to Harry first.

The hours which she had dreaded so were now a golden time, and her heart was singing in her breast. Lyndhurst loved her. She marvelled at the thought. She had not imagined such joy could exist.

She felt as if all her worries had been lifted from her shoulders. Harry could be persuaded, she was sure of it. She had always been able to coax him into her way of thinking in the past.

She bathed her face and hands, and tugged a brush through her flaming curls. Her reflection in the mirror showed her a girl in possession of a wonderful secret. So this was love? She had heard of it, even dreamed of it, but none of the poets she had read had come close to describing the rapture which filled her soul.

Lyndhurst moved towards her as she entered the little parlour, but he did not attempt to take her in his arms. It required iron self-control, but he would keep his part of the bargain, she knew. And it was as well. In his arms she could not trust herself to deny him the answer for which he hoped.

'May I hope that you have regained your appetite?' he said lightly. 'The chef, so I hear, is on his mettle today.'

Rumour had not lied. Georgiana allowed herself to be helped to a delicately flavoured fish soup, followed by a timbale of macaroni *à la napolitaine*. Beef with glazed vegetables followed, and, for the first time in days, she was surprised to find that she could do full justice to the meal. Even so, she was forced to refuse the offer of a charlotte, delicious though it looked.

She had feared at first that after the Viscount's words of love she might feel embarrassed in his presence, but it was not so.

With easy camaraderie he kept the conversation going, avoiding dangerous topics, and speaking only of the country in which they found themselves.

It was clear that he knew it well, and she listened avidly as he told her of the castles of the Loire, the rich countryside of the Dordogne, and the sunbaked beauty of Provence.

'One day I will take you there,' he promised. 'The way of life by the Mediterranean Sea has a subtle charm. The moon is huge, and the nights are warm. It is a land for lovers…'

'My lord, you must not…'

'Georgiana, my name is Edward. Will you not bring yourself to use it? I long to hear it on your lips.'

'Very well, then…Edward. Forgive me, but you have not told me what you mean to do about…about Richard and Harry.' She was loath to break the spell in which he held her, but she had to know his answer.

'I have given it much thought.' He did not seem

irritated by the question. 'Richard, I believe, should be removed from the temptations of city life.

'The fault is mine. I should have seen the danger long ago. Idle hands, a fast set of friends, and no responsibilities… It was a recipe for disaster from the first. I propose to send him out to the West Indies. He may learn to manage my estates.'

'And Harry?' she breathed.

'No, not Harry, my dear. Those two striplings are best apart. But I have an interest in the East India Company. Would he consider a position there?'

A wave of relief swept over Georgiana. 'You are much too good,' she cried warmly. 'Oh, Edward, why did you not tell me of your plans? You led me to believe that you would treat them harshly.'

'They may be glad to put an ocean or two between us when they've heard what I have to say,' he murmured drily. 'But, my dear, I could not tell you what I intended before I was certain of your feelings. I would have you love me on your own account. I had no wish to pressure you by offering to help Harry.'

'And you are certain now?' Long lashes veiled her eyes, but she shot him a slanting glance.

'Yes, my lovely minx, I am quite certain.' His

hand rested lightly on her shoulder, and she felt the warmth through the thin fabric of her gown. 'What a temptress you are! Will you still keep me waiting for my answer?'

Before she could reply Scroggins tapped on the door and entered the room. He bore a message on a silver salver, and the contents caused a frown to crease the Viscount's brow. He muttered something beneath his breath, and ordered his carriage at once.

'I must leave you again, I fear,' he said heavily.

'More mysteries?' Secure in the knowledge of his love, Georgiana smiled as she looked up at him. Nothing could harm her now.

'Nothing too dreadful, I assure you, but my business may take some time.'

'Then I shall have an early night.' She allowed him to kiss her hand, returning the pressure of his fingers with her own.

'Until tomorrow, then?' The deep voice was a caress and she could not mistake the glow of tenderness in his eyes.

'Until tomorrow,' she answered shyly. It was at once a farewell and a promise. Tomorrow she would give him his answers She would agree to become his wife.

Chapter Six

For the rest of that long summer evening Georgiana sat dreaming by her window. As day faded into dusk the western skies were suffused with light from the last rays of the sun. Gold and purple, apricot and magenta streaked the heavens, and the glory of the spectacle seemed to match the rapture in her heart.

She looked about her in wonder. She had not thought that the world could look so different. The chair on which she sat, the small table by her side, even the gleaming flowers of the summer jasmine clinging to the balcony, had taken on a new appearance…a new intensity. She felt that she was seeing them fully for the first time.

Edward loved her. Even now she could not quite

believe it. When had he first known? She could recall each word they had exchanged since their first
meeting. There had been quarrels, misunderstand-
ings, and at times she had hated him. Yet beneath it
all she had never doubted his strength of character.

Was that why she loved him? Now she would
always be cherished and protected by a man who
put his honour above all else. Yet her own security
had never weighed with her.

A little frisson of excitement caused her cheeks
to burn. Life with Edward as her lover would never
be dull. She adored everything about him. A soft
little smile warmed her face. He was infinitely
dear to her.

She stirred impatiently in her chair. She could
not wait to see him again, and from tomorrow she
would not be so cold. She would caress that tousled head as she had always longed to do, and kiss
each finger of those long, graceful hands in turn.

Was it the deep voice that gave him much of his
charm? She could not decide. Perhaps it was the
slow smile which began deep in those clear blue
eyes and grew until it enveloped both of them in a
private world of their own.

A breeze stirred the straying tendrils of her hair,
and she came back to reality with a start. It was

growing chill. She was about to go indoors when she sensed a movement below her balcony. She turned as Harry's head appeared above the balustrade.

His greeting was brief as he stepped into the room and looked about him.

'Where is your bag?' he asked.

'I haven't packed.' Georgiana faced him squarely. 'Harry, we must talk…'

'Not now, for heaven's sake! Georgie, you must see the need for haste, and you promised to be ready…' Muttering beneath his breath, he strode over to a tall chest, opened a drawer, and began to throw her clothing on the bed.

'Wait! I have something to say to you.'

'You may say it whilst you put your things together. Women!' He threw his eyes to the ceiling.

'Sit down!' his sister said quietly. 'This is important.'

Something in her tone made him pause and stare at her. He knew that expression of old. The determined set of her chin convinced him that he had no choice but to listen to her.

He sighed and made an ostentatious show of consulting his watch. 'What is it?' The words were said with an air of patient resignation.

'Harry, we need not leave. Lyndhurst has offered to help both Richard and yourself if you will but agree to meet him.'

Harry's mouth fell open, and for a moment he seemed to have lost the power of speech. Then Georgiana heard an ugly laugh.

'Some hopes of that! Can't you see that he intends to trick you into betraying us? He would say anything to get his way.' A thought struck him and he paled. 'You did not tell him I was coming here tonight?'

'Of course not! But Harry, you are mistaken in him. I do not believe that he means to harm us.' A faint blush coloured her cheeks.

'So that's it!' Harry's sharp eyes had not missed her slight confusion. 'I might have known. Well, he's a plausible devil, I'll give you that. I could tell you stories...'

'Be quiet!' she snapped. 'I will not have you speak ill of him when he thinks only of my...of our welfare.'

'Good God, Georgie, you can't have formed a *tendre* for him? That would be all we need. My dear, there was a woman years ago... Well, all the world knows that he is a brute.'

'I don't believe you.' Georgiana gave him a long considering glance. 'Did you not assure me that the Viscount was too cold a fish ever to look at a woman?' She spoke bravely, but her voice was shaking. She, above anyone, had cause to know of the Viscount's passionate nature.

'I was angry and I lied.' Harry's face was sullen. 'In any case, I did not wish to frighten you. I could not offer to take you away until tonight, but I was worried, Georgie. It was a shock to find you in his company. I hope… Well, I hope that you have not had to suffer his advances…'

'Edward has asked me to be his wife.' The words were out and the silence in the room grew tangible. 'Harry, I love him. Will you not wish me happiness?'

'It would be a waste of breath.' Her brother's expression was remote. 'I can't say that I blame you, though. He will use you ill, but doubtless the rewards will be worth it. They are more than I can offer you.'

Georgiana was shocked by his bitterness, but she would not reproach him.

'I had not considered the rewards, my dear. Is it so strange that I should wish to marry the man who is my happiness?'

'You are deceived in him. This is first love. It's naught but an illusion. You have no experience…'

'I know my own heart.'

'And I no longer have a place in it?'

She detected the undertone of jealousy.

'My dearest, this is different. As for you and me, we shall always be close.' She gave him a pleading smile. 'We have been through so much together.'

'You need not remind me of your sacrifices on my behalf, even if you choose to throw them up at me.'

'I am doing no such thing!' Georgiana finally lost all patience. 'Harry, you are behaving like a spoilt child. Will you not listen to reason for once in your life?'

Her anger jolted him into a new approach.

'I thought I came first in your affections,' he mourned. 'Georgie, you are all I have. How shall I go on without you?'

'You might learn to stand on your own feet,' came the tart reply. 'Edward has offered to find you a place with the East India Company.'

'I won't take his charity.' Harry's sulky expression deepened. 'You shall not sell yourself on my account.'

Georgiana was tempted to slap him, but she forced herself to stay calm.

'It won't be charity,' she said lightly. 'I understand that conditions are hard in India. The agents of the Company earn their stipend, but it would be an adventure. Do you not long to travel to the East?'

She had caught his interest, and he lifted his head.

'Who knows?' she continued with a cheerful smile. 'You might even become a nabob.'

'And Richard will go too?'

Georgiana shook her head. 'Edward hopes that Richard may learn to manage the family estates in the West Indies.'

'I see. He does not trust us together, is that it?' His sneering tone had returned.

'Harry, this is such an opportunity for you. Will you not take it?'

'I can't.' He had turned away from her, his shoulders hunched in despair.

'Why ever not? At least you might discuss it with Edward.'

'Georgie, you don't understand. Even if I cared to face him, it would be useless.'

'I don't see why…'

'Of course you don't see. How could you? If you must have the truth of it, I am not my own master…'

She could only gaze at him in bewilderment.

'What can you mean? The offer has been made to you…'

'And I am not free to take it.'

'My dearest, what on earth is to stop you doing so?'

'Not what, but who.' He could not meet her eyes. 'There is a man... Well, Richard and I are bound to him in a way...'

A chill struck Georgiana to the heart.

'What have you kept from me?' she cried. 'Who is this man?'

'You have seen him,' he said in a low voice. 'You mentioned him to me last night.'

He had no need to go on. Georgiana remembered only too clearly the still, reptilian gaze of the stranger who had watched her so intently.

'What is he to you?' Terror seized her as she waited for his answer.

Harry buried his face in his hands. 'It was he...Merton...who suggested a way of raising money. At first it seemed above-board. Richard and I...well, we had always intended to honour our commitments. Merton was the banker. He's a wealthy man, and he understands finance. It was just that...well, when we needed the money for the annuities we found that it wasn't there.'

'What was his explanation?' A slow tide of anger rose in Georgiana's breast.

'He mentioned bad investments. And, of course, he had given us some of the money as commission.'

'He is more to blame than you,' she cried hotly. 'That a man of his experience should seek to dupe you! Let me tell Edward. He will know what to do. Merton should be prosecuted.'

'He is too clever for that. His name did not appear in any of our dealings.'

'No matter! Edward will challenge him and force him to return the money.'

'No!' Harry's voice had risen to a shout and for the first time she saw real fear in his eyes. 'Keep Lyndhurst out of this as you value his life. You do not know Merton. He has threatened to kill us if we betray him, and he will keep his word.'

Georgiana needed no convincing. At first sight she had sensed an aura of evil about the mysterious stranger. Her brain was reeling, but she would not give up hope of saving Harry.

'Then you have all the more reason for leaving for the East,' she cried. 'He cannot trace you there, nor would he find Richard in the West Indies.'

'We should never reach the ship.' Harry was very pale. 'Merton has spies... He would murder us without compunction.'

'Even if you promised him your silence? I give you my word that I shall not mention him to Edward, though I should dearly love to do so.'

'He would laugh in your face. Besides, he has other plans for us.'

Her fear now matched his own as she looked at his bent head. She tried to speak, but at first the words would not come.

'Tell me!' she forced out at last.

'He intends to set us up in another city.' Harry would not meet her eyes. 'We can still be useful to him. People trust us, you see, and Merton will not give up the chance of more rich pickings.'

'You shall not do it,' Georgiana said with decision. 'You must have nothing more to do with him. Let him try to harm you and Edward will—'

'Lyndhurst cannot protect us every moment of the day and night. Will you risk his life too?'

Her silence gave him his answer. He rose to his feet, swept her clothing together, and crammed it into her bag.

'I won't go with you.' She snatched it from him. 'Have you thought at all about our future? Are we to live the life of criminals, with the thought of capture always in our minds?'

'I have thought of nothing else.' His face revealed his agony of mind. 'But Georgie, you must come with me. Merton has seen you. He feels that you…'

'That I will help to dupe his victims?' She saw from his expression that she was right. 'I won't do it, Harry.'

'It was not a suggestion. Merton has made up his mind.'

'Then let him try to take me. I promise you he will regret it.'

'And so would you. You have not seen him in a rage. I do not believe him to be quite normal.'

'Splendid!' In her fear and rage Georgiana lashed out at him. 'A lunatic? How carefully you choose your friends, my dear!'

'Georgie, don't.' Harry took her hands in his. 'If we go together now we may yet find a way to escape him.'

'Very well.' She felt as if her heart had turned to stone as she made the decision, but she could see no alternative. She would risk neither Harry's life nor Edward's, though she was throwing away her only hope of happiness.

If she left now, Edward would think that she had gone of her own free will. He would never trust her again. All his previous suspicions would be confirmed, and he would despise her even more for the false promise of love she had offered.

An iron band of anguish constricted her chest

as she took a last look around the pretty room. At that moment she felt that her life was over.

Harry was already at the door. He seemed to be waiting for a signal of some kind. Then he beckoned.

'The coast is clear. Make haste.' As he hurried her towards the back staircase a door closed quietly in the corridor. She looked round fearfully, but there was no sign of the mysterious stranger.

They gained the street without detection, and he hurried her into the waiting coach. Harry drew the curtains closed, but not before she had caught a glimpse of the Viscount strolling towards the hotel in company with another man.

Lyndhurst was resplendent in full evening dress. The perfectly fitting coat set off his broad shoulders to advantage, and Brummell himself could not have bettered the cut of the black satin breeches which clung closely to his long legs. As he passed within a yard of where she sat he turned to his companion with the smile she loved so well. She heard his deep voice though she could not distinguish his words.

The temptation to call out to him was almost irresistible, but she fought back a cry of panic. The knuckles shone white on her clenched fists. Then

Harry tapped on the roof of the coach, the driver whipped up the horses, and the moment was gone.

Hot tears coursed down Georgiana's cheeks as the vehicle gathered speed, putting more distance between herself and the man she loved. How cruel it was to have her happiness snatched away. In that moment she hated Harry.

As if he sensed her feelings he turned to her.

'Will you ever forgive me? I did not intend…'

'You never do,' she cried wildly. 'Don't speak to me, or I might say something that we shall both regret.'

Her bitter words silenced him. She was shivering, though the night was warm, and wordlessly he threw a rug about her knees.

When the coach drew to a halt he handed her down. Money changed hands. Then he took her arm and led her across the street to where another vehicle waited in the shadows. It appeared to be of ancient vintage.

'Where have you been?' Richard jumped down from the box. 'I have waited here this age.'

'Keep your voice down,' Harry ordered. 'You'll wake the neighbourhood. Now let us away before we are pursued.'

A short altercation followed as both of them

wished to drive. Eventually Richard returned to his perch and took the reins. He set off at such an alarming rate that Georgiana protested.

'Do beg him to slow down,' she pleaded. 'If he overturns us we shall be in worse case than ever.'

'Don't fuss, Georgie! You were not used to be such a namby-pamby miss.'

'Hal, I mean it! Tell him to slow down.'

'Richard can handle the ribbons,' Harry told her in an injured tone. 'He's had plenty of practice up and down the public roads in England. For a guinea or two the mail-coach drivers will give up their place to anyone.'

Georgiana shuddered at the thought of coach and passengers in such inexperienced hands. She refused to be convinced.

'Oh, very well. I'll sit beside him.' Harry thrust his head out of the window and called out. He was unprepared for what happened next.

Alarmed by his shout, Richard snatched so sharply at the reins that the horses reared in pain and fright. Georgiana was flung across the coach to the opposite seat, bruising her arms and knees as she fell. It was the outside of enough.

'Get out!' she ordered, and Harry obeyed her, dreading the storm which he knew must follow.

She did not mince her words, and spoke with a force which left both of her companions much subdued. Then she climbed back inside The outburst of anger had relieved her feelings, but she could not shake off a deadening sense of depression. Had not Edward told her once that she was taking on a task beyond her power when she tried to help her brother? She was beginning to believe him.

Suddenly she longed with passion for Lyndhurst's calm good sense. If only he were by her side she would fear nothing and no one. She forced the thought away. She must not dwell on those precious hours in the shelter of his arms, else her courage would fail her.

She looked about her with distaste. The musty smell inside the coach was sickening. Even in the half-light she could see that the padding was almost gone from the seats, and the leather itself was ripped.

What had happened to their family coach? she wondered. In this ramshackle contraption Harry could scarce hope to reach Paris, and Italy would be out of the question.

In great discomfort she suffered the jolting for what seemed like hours. They were travelling more slowly, but it was a relief when Richard brought the coach to a stop. The sound of another argument did not improve her temper.

'Twenty miles is far enough, I tell you.' Harry's voice was raw with strain. 'These broken-down nags will not go further.'

'You chose them,' Richard said sulkily.

'They were all we could afford.'

'I know it, but perhaps at the next inn…'

'They won't do it. Do you want them dropping in their traces?'

Richard made no reply. Muttering under his breath, he climbed down from the box, and together they made their way into the hostelry.

Georgiana was glad to stretch her legs. She felt stiff and sore, and the constant quarrelling had increased her worries. She had not expected perfect accord, but to disagree so soon…? It did not augur well.

After they had ordered refreshments, Harry engaged the landlord in conversation, but when he came back to them he was frowning.

'There are no horses to be had,' he said shortly. 'We are not the first to take this route tonight. We had best bait our own and trust to luck.'

'Did I not tell you so?' Richard's smug expression was infuriating. In triumph he ordered a second bottle of claret.

Georgiana sipped at her coffee. She was more anxious than she dared admit. She feared an explosion of anger if she objected, but when the second bottle was empty and a third ordered she felt it was time to protest.

'Had you not best keep your wits about you?' she murmured. 'The horses are tired, and we do not know the road.'

Harry flushed, but before he could speak Richard intervened.

'We must rest the nags,' he explained kindly. She might have been a backward child, to judge by his tone. 'Pray don't trouble yourself. Why, I have seen drivers so disguised that they could scarce hold the ribbons. It happens frequently. These horses know their way.'

'Stuff! I value my neck if you do not.' She turned to her brother. 'Why are we travelling thus? Where is our own coach?'

Harry had the grace to blush. 'We...er...needed funds, my dear.'

'Could you not ask your friend?' Her voice was heavy with sarcasm. If Merton intended to use them for his own ends, at least he might help them travel in comfort.

'I would not do so.' Harry's face was set, and

she did not pursue the subject, though Richard had left them to order the horses put to.

When he returned she knew at once that something was wrong.

'Here's a pretty pass,' he cried. 'One of the wheels is gone.'

'Gone?' Harry stared at him.

'It is broken clean away. Did I not warn you when you bought the coach? Any fool could have seen…'

'Shut up!' Harry was furious. 'If you recall, you had no wish to stop here. If I'd listened to you we might have found ourselves overturned in some God-forsaken spot—'

'Be quiet, both of you!' Georgiana turned on them, her eyes flashing with anger. 'Will quarrelling solve the problem? For heaven's sake use your heads! There must be someone…a carpenter perhaps?'

'It will take two days.' Thoroughly dispirited, Richard sank into a chair. 'We cannot wait so long.'

'I'll see to it.' Harry stalked off, and after a moment or two Richard followed him.

She was out of all patience with the pair of them. Why was she travelling with these two feckless idiots? If only she'd followed her instinct to tell Edward.

She straightened her shoulders. There was no use in repining. She had made her decision and she must abide by it, though with every hour that passed she recognised her own folly even more.

Worse was yet to come.

When the two men returned Harry laid a purse beside her.

'What is this?'

'You will need the gold for your journey, Georgie.' He looked uncomfortable.

'For *my* journey? What do you mean?'

'We...er...thought you might be more comfortable in the public coach,' Richard offered. 'We cannot stay here in case we are followed.'

'Georgie, we'll take the nags and go ahead to Paris,' Harry said quickly. 'This place is on a public route. You won't have long to wait for the coach, and you will be quite safe. I'll speak to the landlord.'

Rage threatened to choke her, and her look was withering. She could not trust herself to answer him.

'Don't look like that,' Harry pleaded. 'You must agree that it is for the best. Go to the Hôtel Belle Ile in Paris. We'll see you there tonight.'

'It was not our fault, you know.' Richard attempted to placate her. 'It was naught but ill luck.'

'I'll be happy to explain that to your brother if he comes in search of you.' She was unable to resist the taunt and Richard coloured to the ears. She turned away as Harry attempted to kiss her farewell. He shifted uneasily from one foot to the other. Then he sighed and walked away.

Alone with her bitter thoughts, she fell prey once more to her doubts and fears. She was certain of nothing. She might have been upon shifting sands, unable to trust the very ground beneath her feet. The void which had opened before her filled her with despair. What on earth was she to do? Harry could not protect her, she knew that now.

In an agony of mind, she rested her burning face against the cool glass of the window. Outside it was full daylight. In Calais Edward would be awake... She wondered if she had been missed already. There was little doubt of it. Betsy would have given the alarm when she found her mistress vanished.

Georgiana shuddered as she imagined her lover's reaction to the news. He had trusted her and she had betrayed his trust. There was no sign of a struggle in her room. It would be clear that she had left of her own free will. Free will? A bitter smile curved her lips. She had had little choice.

She looked at her watch. There were still some hours to wait before the public coach arrived, and the inn was growing crowded as prospective passengers arrived.

As the noise increased she put up the hood of her cloak, drawing it about her face. She longed to ask for a private room, but that would deplete her meagre funds. She picked up a nearby broadsheet, pretending to be absorbed in it, but her command of French was limited, and the contents did not interest her. Her thoughts returned to her present problems.

She had not been kind to Harry, she thought sadly, but really his behaviour was the outside of enough. He seemed to stumble from one disaster to another. What had happened to the laughing boy she had always loved so much? It did not seem possible that he would leave her here alone.

A burst of laughter from a group of men nearby caused her to lift her head. Then one of them left his friends and came towards her.

'All alone, *mademoiselle?* Will you take a glass with me?'

Georgiana eyed him with distaste. Burly and red-faced, he was old enough to be her father. She gave him a quelling look and turned away.

Taking her silence for assent, he lifted a hand to summon the landlord. 'Wine for the little lady and myself,' he ordered.

Georgiana rose at once, intending to change her seat, but he grasped her arm, forcing her to sit beside him.

'Sir, I am waiting for my friends,' she said with dignity.

'They are over-long in arriving. I've watched you for an hour or more. Now don't be unfriendly, my dear. I've a wager against your kindness.'

Georgiana looked round for the landlord, but he was occupied in serving. She raised an arm to attract his attention.

'Now, now,' her tormentor soothed. 'I mean you no harm.' He glanced towards his erstwhile companions with a grin, nodding to the circle of expectant faces.

'How dare you speak to me?' she hissed. 'Release my arm or I'll make a scene which you won't forget.'

It was the wrong thing to say. Her companion crimsoned. With a swift motion of his hand he threw back her hood.

'A hell-cat, but a beauty too,' he marvelled. Before she could pull away from him he slid an arm about her waist.

'Just one kiss?' he insisted. 'You'll never miss it.'

She swung round then, intending to slap his face, but he was too quick for her. His other hand came down upon her shoulder, forcing her back into her seat and ripping the thin muslin of her gown.

His eyes glistened as they feasted on the smooth expanse of milky flesh. As he bent his face to hers he was breathing hard. She struggled wildly as the slobbering mouth came closer, to the accompaniment of shouts and laughter from his friends.

Then she heard a choking gasp. The man's hands flew to his throat as his eyes began to bulge and his face grew purple. As she watched in horror he was lifted from his seat and flung to the ground.

Half strangled, her attacker tried to crawl away. He was helped along by a swift kick from a booted foot.

Georgiana stared up at the owner of the boot and found herself gazing into Lyndhurst's face. He was very pale, but the blue eyes blazed with anger.

Chapter Seven

A lifted finger brought the landlord to his side. Her command of French was not enough to enable her to follow all he said, but it sufficed to reduce the man to a quivering jelly.

Lyndhurst had not looked at her, but now he took her arm in a brutal grip and marched her through the rapidly thinning crowd. In silence he thrust her ahead of him in the wake of their abject host, and pushed her into a private room.

'Out!' He jerked his head, and the man scuttled off like a frightened rabbit. Then he turned to Georgiana and she quailed at his expression, though his look was impersonal. She might have been a stranger.

'Where are they?' Somehow the quiet tone was

more menacing than if he had stormed at her and she began to tremble.

'Edward, please let me explain!'

'More words, Miss Westleigh? I don't wish to hear them, though you have a gifted tongue. I should not believe you now if you swore on the Bible.'

'You are quick to judge me,' she cried on a sob.

'Spare me your tears. They will not move me. You will give me your brother's direction, if you please.'

'He and Richard are gone,' she faltered. 'You don't understand. They are in danger. Harry told me...'

Lyndhurst's face was thunderous. 'Gone? Do you tell me that they left you here alone?'

'They had no choice. The coach broke down and it could not be repaired...'

'And with your brother's usual tender care for your safety he abandoned you to the mercies of any ill-favoured lout who cares to approach you? It does not surprise me in the least.'

'They...they suggested that I wait for the public coach. Harry spoke with the landlord. He was to see that I was not...not molested.'

'A task which he performed with great efficiency, I note,' Lyndhurst's voice was silky. 'No private room, Miss Westleigh? Your brother must have left you well provided with funds.'

Georgiana's hand closed convulsively on the small bag of coins in her reticule, but Lyndhurst was quick...uncomfortably quick. He took the purse from her nerveless fingers, opened it, and shook out the contents on to the table.

'A fortune indeed!' he observed in a sarcastic tone. 'At least enough to take you on to Paris. And what then?'

Frightened, exhausted and faint from lack of food, Georgiana burst into tears. For a few moments the silence of the room was broken only by her sobbing.

'I will send Betsy to you,' Lyndhurst said abruptly. 'She will help you repair your gown. Then we go on.'

Georgiana felt that her heart must break. She was still in tears when Betsy tapped at the door.

'There, miss, don't take on so.' She threw a comforting arm around Georgiana's shoulders.

'I...I shall be better in a moment.'

'Of course you will. Master has got hisself in a state... He don't know what he's saying, and that's the truth.'

'He...he has every right to be cross.' Georgiana dabbed at her eyes.

'Cross? Miss, he were like a madman when he found you'd gone. We've fairly flown along that road from Calais. I can still feel the bumps.' She rubbed at her hip with a rueful expression.

'I'm very glad to see you,' Georgiana said in a small voice. 'And Betsy, I hope I did not get you into trouble with his lordship.'

'No! He cursed everything and everybody alike, but it weren't meant for me in particler. Will I take a needle to the rip in your gown, miss?'

Georgiana sat in silence as the girl drew the edges of the fabric together.

'It don't show much,' Betsy announced with satisfaction. She turned as a servant entered the room.

'Take it away.' Georgiana waved aside the tray of food.

'Leave it!' Lyndhurst was standing in the doorway. The look on his face was enough to send both Betsy and the waiter scurrying from the room.

'Miss Westleigh, you will eat, or I shall feed you forcibly.' It was clear that he meant what he said.

Miserably, she forced down a few mouthfuls of the food, though she felt that it must choke her.

Lyndhurst did not address her further, but when she had finished he held out her cloak.

In stony silence he led her out to the waiting coach, leaving it to Scroggins to hand her inside.

Neither Betsy nor her uncle dared to speak as they continued on the road to Paris, and after one quick glance at the Viscount's grim expression Georgiana thought it wise to follow their example. His contempt for her was apparent in every line of his rigid frame, and she could only wish that the ground would open and swallow her. She had never been so miserable in her life.

At the end of that dreadful journey he addressed her once. 'The name of your meeting place?' he demanded.

'The Hôtel Belle Ile.'

Without another word, he marched her to her room. It was commodious, but she was quick to notice that there was no balcony. She looked round in surprise as the servants brought in an extra bed.

Lyndhurst answered her unspoken question. 'Betsy will also sleep in here,' he said.

'As my gaoler? I won't have it!' In her misery and frustration Georgiana screamed at him.

'You have no choice, Miss Westleigh. It is either Betsy or myself.'

'You...you hypocrite! You pretend to be scandalised because my brother left me, and now you will take advantage...'

'You flatter yourself. Experience has taught me well. I have not the slightest desire for your company, but you shall not make a fool of me again.'

Hot colour flooded her cheeks, but he affected not to notice.

'Who is it to be?' he demanded. 'Betsy or myself?'

'Need you ask?' She eyed him with a mixture of anger and despair. 'As you find my company so distasteful you may send Betsy to me.'

He bowed, but before he left her he spoke again. 'May I offer you a word of warning? Betsy has her orders. Should anyone approach you, or should you try to leave this room, I shall hear of it at once.'

Her silence was eloquent as she turned her back on him.

'I shall be close at hand,' he continued. 'The adjoining door leads to my rooms.'

'Perhaps you would care to chain my hands and feet?' she cried bitterly.

'It would be no more than you deserve.' He was about to leave her when she turned and threw out her hands to him.

'Edward, will you not listen to me?' she pleaded. 'I had no wish to steal away without a word to you, but Harry told me something…'

He gave a cynical laugh. 'Harry again? When will you learn that your brother will tell you anything to gain his own ends? I suppose he does not care to lose the most valuable member of his infamous group.'

'I thought you fair-minded,' she burst out in rage. 'You won't even listen to what I have to say.'

'Another tissue of lies? You are right. I do not care to listen. You cannot distinguish right from wrong.'

The bitter words struck her to the heart, but she did not reply. It was useless. Nothing she could say or do would make him trust her again. She walked over to the window, hiding her face from him. She would not give him the satisfaction of seeing how cruelly he had wounded her. When she turned round at last she was alone.

A deadly lassitude settled on her spirits. She had achieved nothing by agreeing to Harry's plan. In fact, she had made matters worse if anything. Now she was virtually a prisoner.

She saw nothing of Lyndhurst for the rest of the day, and as the hours passed her apprehension grew. Harry would know by now that she had not taken the public coach. Would he guess that the Viscount had found her? And what of Merton? The thought of that sinister figure made her shudder. She could imagine his rage when he found that his plans had gone awry. If only Edward would listen to her.

Her hopes were vain. On the following day she was allowed out for a short drive, with Scroggins and Betsy in attendance. Lyndhurst sat aloft with his coachman. He neither looked at nor spoke to her. She might have been a leper, she thought sadly. It was clear that he could not bear the sight of her.

She dined alone and the hours dragged endlessly. The solitude weighed heavily on her spirits, but as the day wore on her indignation grew. She was being treated like a child, punished by being sent to her room. The thought served to stiffen her resolve.

When she next saw the Viscount she would give him a piece of her mind. There were laws against abduction, for a nobleman no less than a commoner. He had no right to hold her against her will.

When the door opened she swung round with flashing eyes, but her expression softened when she saw that it was Betsy. The girl looked nervous as she sidled into the room. She reached into her pocket and thrust a note into Georgiana's hand.

'Where did you get this?' Georgiana snatched at the folded paper.

'A man gave it to me. I knowed it was your brother, miss. His hair was the colour of yours. I told him I wasn't supposed to fetch it to you, but he said that my master should not keep you from your family.' She twisted her hands in her apron. 'Oh, miss, you won't tell his lordship, will you? He'd skin me alive.'

Georgiana laid a comforting hand on Betsy's arm and shook her head. The contents of the note were brief. Harry counselled patience. He would find a way to help her escape from Lyndhurst. She sighed. At least he had discovered her whereabouts.

She looked at Betsy's anxious face. 'It is nothing,' she said lightly. 'My brother was worried, but now he knows that I am here. I'm glad to hear from him.'

'Is that all?' Betsy's smile lacked much of its normal gaiety. 'I was that afeared that he'd take you off again.'

'Oh, Betsy, I am so sorry. I did not mean to get

you into trouble with your master. It was not your fault that I left without...without saying anything. The Viscount must know that.'

'You wouldn't have thought so, miss.' Betsy's lip quivered. 'If I hadn't come to your room right early, to see if you wanted me, we might not have knowed till noon.'

'Betsy, I had to go. I'll tell you about it some time.'

Betsy glanced towards the window. 'He...your brother...asked me if you had a balcony.' Her eyes began to sparkle. 'He's brave, Miss Georgiana. To think how he climbed up to see you! But how did you get down? His lordship went mad when he saw the broken creeper. He said you were like to have killed yourself.'

'I left by the staircase,' Georgiana said with dignity.

'Well, my master didn't know that. You should have seen him... The hotel was in an uproar. When he couldn't find you we were out of Calais before you could say knife.' She forbore to mention the Viscount's promises of retribution.

A peremptory knock at the door startled both of them. It could only be Lyndhurst.

'Quick! Help me out of my gown before you

open the door.' Georgiana stuffed the note in her pocket. 'Betsy, you must say that I have retired.'

The knock was repeated.

'One moment!' Georgiana called.

The door was thrown open and the Viscount entered.

'I believe I asked you to wait.' She rounded on him with an angry look, drawing her wrapper close about her.

Lyndhurst ignored her protest. He stood very still in the centre of the room, glancing from one face to the other.

'Betsy?' He turned and held the door wide. The girl need no second bidding to leave the room.

'Please go!' Georgiana turned back to her mirror and began to brush her hair. 'It is late, and, as you see, I intend to seek my bed.'

'Alone? Such a pity! And such a waste!' He had walked across the room and was standing behind her. Reaching out, he twisted a copper curl around his fingers.

In a furious gesture she slapped his hand away. She tried to rise, but his hands came down upon her shoulders, holding her in an iron grip. Even through the flimsy robe she could feel their warmth. It seemed to burn into her flesh.

Panic threatened to overwhelm her. He hated her, she knew that now. Did he intend to take his revenge by raping her? She must stay calm. If she struggled or showed her fear he would enjoy his triumph even more.

'I believe you have dined too well, my lord. You are not yourself, else you would not insult me so.'

'Insult you? Is that possible?' His eyes were glittering with an emotion she did not recognise, but she forced herself not to shrink from him.

She was in no doubt of his intentions, but he would not take her without a struggle. She would need all her wits about her. The love which she had been so ready to offer him should not be debased into a mere animal coupling.

'Abduction and now rape, my lord? You value your honour lightly. As I recall you told me once that you would never force a woman.'

'I have changed, my dear. My honour has been flung back in my face. You will pay for that. As you say, I have dined well, but not too well to do you justice.'

'You disgust me!'

'The feeling is mutual as far as character is concerned, yet there are other consolations...' His hand slid the robe aside, exposing the milky smoothness of her shoulder.

Rigid with anger, she stared into the mirror as he bent and pressed his lips against her flesh. Then he lifted her to her feet, and turned her round to face him. With a soft whisper of silk her robe fell to the ground.

Clad only in her petticoat, Georgiana stood straight and still. Proudly she raised her head and looked at her erstwhile lover. She was very pale, and the great green eyes were huge in her set face.

'I was mistaken in you. You called me a liar and a cheat. Are you any better than I? Worse, I think. What I have done I did for love of my brother. You, my lord, are filled with hatred and self-pity. Take me if you must. I wish you joy of the experience.'

Lyndhurst's face flushed darkly at her stinging words. With a muttered curse he flung her from him and stormed out of the room.

She found that she was trembling as if she had the ague. She stumbled towards the bed, and lay there inert. Was this the man she had vowed to love with all her heart? He could have wounded her no more cruelly if he had raped her there and then. Her hands were like ice. With shaking fingers she pulled the coverlet about her.

He had done her one service, at least. Now she would have no compunction about leaving him. She would live up to his expectations. If she must lie and cheat to get away she would do so. Nothing must be allowed to stand in her way.

Let Merton do his worst. Even his company seemed preferable to that of the man who had just left her. She closed her eyes, but it was almost dawn before she fell asleep.

'Miss, are you all right?' Betsy looked troubled by her mistress's appearance on the following day.

'Quite well, I thank you.' Georgiana managed the briefest of smiles, but Betsy was not reassured.

'You look…different, somehow…not quite yourself.'

'I have been too much indoors.'

'His lordship was saying as much. He's waiting to see you, miss…in the parlour.'

Georgiana marched through at once, to find Lyndhurst standing by the window, apparently lost in thought.

As she entered the room he turned and came towards her.

'Georgiana, I…'

A lifted hand stopped the flow of words. 'Don't

trouble to apologise, my lord. You will not change my opinion of your behaviour.' Her voice was icy. 'You have some instructions for me?'

'None… Will you please listen?'

'As readily as you were prepared to listen to me?'

He winced. 'I deserved that. But, my dear, I was out of my mind with worry. You can have no idea of the danger to which you might have been exposed.'

'I know it now!' She faced him proudly. 'My safety is at much at risk with you as with any other man.'

'That is not true.' He attempted to take her hand. 'I am not made of stone, Georgiana, and you are a very beautiful woman, but I would not harm you.'

'I don't believe you.'

She saw the hurt in his eyes, and the shame. Now, when he was at her feet, was the time to tell him the full story, but anger kept her silent. She would never forgive him. With a stony expression she turned away.

'May I go now?' she asked in a toneless voice.

'Of course. You need not ask my permission. I wish I could make you see why it is necessary to keep you in this place.'

'There is no need to explain. I understand perfectly. I am the bait...the tethered goat. When your victims come to find me you will seize them.'

Lyndhurst realised that he could expect no softening of her attitude. 'Did you tell these so-called victims of my plans for them?' he asked abruptly.

For the first time Georgiana wavered. If she told the truth she would be forced to explain that Harry and Richard were linked inextricably with Merton. She could imagine the outcome. Lyndhurst would seek out that sinister figure, putting himself at risk.

It was no concern of hers, of course. She did not care what happened to him. A vision of his lifeless corpse came unbidden to her mind, and an expression of horror crossed her face. She would not be a party to murder.

'No!' she answered firmly.

'You are the poorest of liars, my dear. Look at me!' Blue eyes locked with green ones. 'There is something wrong, is there not? What had they to say?'

'They did not wish to do as you suggested.' The excuse would serve for the moment, and she prayed that he would not press her further.

'I see.' Lyndhurst looked thoughtful. 'In that case there is no more to be said.' He changed the subject. 'Do you care to take a drive this morning?'

'Why not? The bait must be well advertised, I believe. Doubtless Harry will recognise your carriage and guess that I am here.'

'That was not my first intention. If you must have the truth, you do not look at all the thing…'

'And you are surprised? You astonish me, my lord! Strange though it may seem to you, I am unaccustomed to defending my honour against a brute.'

Lyndhurst's face grew dark. 'I shall trouble you no further, madam.' He gave her a formal bow and walked towards the door.

'Wait!' Georgiana's mind was racing. Harry might be awaiting just this opportunity to rescue her. Indoors she was kept close, but if she could persuade Lyndhurst to walk with her, rather than take the carriage… In the narrow streets of Paris she might slip away from him.

She prayed that Harry was watching the hotel, for she had no desire to find herself alone in a strange city.

'I find myself in need of air, though I have no wish to drive,' she said. 'Perhaps a walk?'

Lyndhurst's face cleared. He came towards her with an eager look, but her cold expression stopped him.

'Pray do not imagine that I seek your company. Your presence is abhorrent to me. You will keep your distance, sir.'

'As you wish.' From the look of pain which crossed his face she might have struck him.

There was silence between them as they strolled towards the river in the summer sunshine. Paris was looking at its best, but Georgiana could find no pleasure in the fine buildings, the avenues of spreading trees, and the bustling crowds about her.

Two lovers came towards them, their faces bright with happiness. This was a city for lovers, someone had told her long ago. She could not help but contrast the joy of others with her own despair. Things might have been so different...

She was intensely aware of the man beside her, and of the glances which he attracted from the women who strolled past them with their escorts. She glared fiercely as she caught a smile or an inviting look, and was mortified when she heard laughter as they passed.

They thought her jealous, and it infuriated her. She was nothing of the kind. They did nit know the Viscount as she did. His striking appearance was a sham.

As always he was perfectly attired, the blue coat

of Bath superfine sitting to advantage on his broad shoulders. He was taller than the men about him, his long legs encased in spotless buckskins. She did not need the lascivious looks to assure her that those heavily muscled calves were unpadded.

I would wish them joy of him, she thought savagely. She alone knew of the false promise in those brilliant eyes. That mobile mouth could spit venom when he chose, and tenderness could turn in a moment to unbridled lust. He would have taken her out of hatred. That she could not forgive.

The thought served to stiffen her resolve. She straightened her shoulders. The past could not be changed. Now she must think of the future. She glanced about her. Figures stirred in the deep shadow of the buildings, but she saw no sign of Harry. She was forced to pause as Lyndhurst threw a coin to a crippled beggar, but no help was at hand.

The cripple shuffled forward until he was directly in their path. 'Blessings on your kind heart, my lord.'

Georgiana's heart was stirred as she looked at him. He'd been sitting on the pavement with outstretched legs. His feet were bare of shoes or stockings, and at first glance it seemed strange that someone of his powerful build should be reduced to begging.

Then she looked at his arms. They were raised in supplication, and with a start she realised that he had no hands. The arms had been severed at the elbows.

Perilously close to tears, she reached into her reticule, but as she bent towards the man she noticed that his eyes were bright.

'Same time tomorrow...at this place?' The words were so low that she could barely catch them.

As she handed him a coin she nodded, glad to see that Lyndhurst had moved on ahead of her. He stopped and turned. Then something in her face caused him to take her arm.

'You are distressed,' he murmured. 'That is a tragic sight, but sadly it is all too common since the recent wars. One sees so much of it in England.'

'Poor fellows!' She allowed him to lead her away. He had not heard the muttered message; that much was clear. With an effort she tried to compose herself. The man's words had been unexpected, and they had shaken her.

'Will you sit down?' Lyndhurst led her to a nearby seat. 'Strange, is it not, that some regard these men as parasites? To relieve their poverty in any way is thought to encourage them in idleness.'

'Better to give to nine undeserving cases for the sake of the tenth who may need help.'

'I agree, yet there are problems. Many of these unfortunates can get no work. If they would eat they must turn to robbery or worse.'

'It is unjust!' she cried. 'The man back there…the cripple…how could he earn his bread?'

'In the only way he knows; he must beg.' Lyndhurst frowned. 'It is a poor reward for bravery.'

'Can nothing be done for them?' Georgiana had forgotten her resolve to keep her companion at a distance. Her face was alight with indignation as she turned to him.

'I fear not. There are thousands in similar case. In England we try… Well, I must not trouble you further with sad tales.'

'Yet his eyes were so bright,' Georgiana murmured. 'I wish…'

'May I give you a word of warning, Georgiana? The man's injuries were shocking, and you will see others in the streets of Paris. Compassion should not blind you to the fact that some of these beggars are dangerous.'

Startled, she rose to her feet. Had he heard the message after all?

'No, don't run away. There is no need to be frightened. You are safe with me. I meant merely that it is not wise to approach such men unless you are well protected.'

'A man without hands? How could he harm me?' she asked scornfully.

'He could trip you for the benefit of his friends. You did not notice? There were others in the background...'

'And I thought you sympathised with him...'

'Pity mingled with caution, my dear. I have seen the lengths to which starving men will go. I don't blame them. In similar circumstances I might do the same.'

'At least you are no hypocrite, my lord.' The words were out before she could consider their possible effect. She had spoken on impulse, and she realised her mistake at once. Lyndhurst took her hand in his.

'Thank you, Georgiana.' His keen eyes searched her face intently. Then he sighed. 'We had best go back. It is growing chill.'

Was it a reference to the fact that she had resumed her unyielding manner towards him? Her lips tightened. She must not weaken now. How close she had come to slipping back into their old relationship... For a few moments she had forgotten how much she despised him.

Yet it was hard to resist his charm. For the rest of the day he was attentive, amusing her with his conversation, and affecting not to notice that her replies were brief.

To throw him off guard she needed guile, and as the hours slipped by she allowed herself to respond more easily. When he left her that evening the look of strain had vanished from his expression, and she was satisfied with her own deception. At all costs she must persuade him to walk with her on the following day.

Lyndhurst fell in at once with her suggestion. As they strolled along the boulevards the next morning he looked so cheerful that her heart misgave her. A knot of anxiety formed in her breast. She had no idea what was to happen when they reached the beggar's corner.

Would Harry arrange some incident to draw Lyndhurst from her side? She glanced at the tall figure beside her. Surely they would not harm him? Her footsteps began to lag.

'Come, my lady of mercy! Did you not tell me that you wished to help the cripple further?' Lyndhurst gave her a fond glance. 'I believe you would like to start a home for such as he.'

She gave him a faint smile, which vanished as

they turned the corner. The cripple was in his usual place, and Georgiana began to tremble.

'Do you stay here. I will give him something.' Lyndhurst released her arm and walked over to the man. Then the alleyway erupted as men came running from the shadows.

A raised cudgel caught Lyndhurst on the shoulder, sending him reeling against the wall. He turned with catlike speed, but he had no weapon, and his fists were of little use against his heavily armed attackers.

As Georgiana watched in horror he went down beneath a flailing mass of bodies. Then she heard a shot. As if by magic the beggars melted away, and Georgiana flew to Lyndhurst's side.

He was still conscious, thought his face was bleeding. As she bent over him he looked beyond her.

'I thank you, sir,' he said with a rueful smile.

Georgiana turned, and then she gasped. Merton was looking down at her. Carefully, he replaced the pistol in his cloak, and reached out a hand to help Lyndhurst to his feet.

Chapter Eight

'You came at an opportune moment, sir.' Lyndhurst was breathing fast. 'This lady and I are in your debt.'

'It was nothing. I was glad to be of some small service to you.' Merton held out his hand as he introduced himself. Then he turned to Georgiana. 'Madam is unharmed, I trust?'

Stupefied, Georgiana could only stare at him.

'The lady appears to be badly shocked, my lord. May I suggest that you make use of my carriage?' He lifted his heavy walking cane to summon a coach which was waiting lower down the street. 'Where are you staying, sir?'

'At the Belle Ile.' Tenderly the Viscount lifted Georgiana in his arms and carried her to the vehicle.

'A lucky coincidence…I am staying there myself.' Merton settled himself in the opposite seat. 'Sir, you are bleeding. You will frighten the lady.' He proffered a snowy handkerchief.

'Miss Westleigh is made of stern stuff.' Lyndhurst held her close within the circle of his arm. 'But had those villains reached her… Lord Merton, I can only blame myself. It was folly to venture forth unarmed.'

'You had no cause to expect an attack, I imagine.' Merton's eyes rested on Georgiana's face with interest. 'No warning…?'

'None at all. Miss Westleigh wished to see something of the city…and we had spoken to one of the beggars yesterday. She hoped to help him in some way.'

'A sad mistake.' Merton shook his head. 'These fellows are no better than animals. Like wild beasts, they will turn and rend you. The lady will have learned her lesson.'

Georgiana could not mistake his meaning. He had made it clear that Lyndhurst's life was at his mercy. Without his intervention, her lover would now be a bloody corpse. She could not begin to understand this terrifying creature. With Lyndhurst unconscious he might have spirited her away. Why had he not done so?

As is he had read her mind Merton gave her a wolfish smile. 'No harm done,' he announced smoothly. 'Those simple-minded fellows sought nothing more than a fat purse. How pleasant it must be to have one's desires satisfied so easily.'

Georgiana could not take her eyes from him. She felt held by that silver gaze. He might have been a coiled snake and she the intended victim. That he had arranged the attack on Lyndhurst she had no doubt, but why had he come to their rescue?

Whatever the reason, she could only be thankful that Lyndhurst had escaped his attackers with nothing more than a cut on his brow. She looked up at him with anxious eyes, relieved to see that the bleeding had stopped. He met her look with a wry smile.

'The price of folly,' he announced lightly. Then he turned to Merton. 'Sir, do you care to dine with us this evening…that is, unless you are otherwise engaged?'

Georgiana's blood ran cold. She laid a restraining hand upon his arm. 'Edward, would it not be best—?'

'Madam is concerned for your health, my lord. She may be right. You have sustained a blow… Neglect of such an injury will often lead to serious consequences.' She heard the mockery in his voice, but Lyndhurst seemed unaware of it.

'It is but a graze.' He renewed his invitation.

'You are quite sure?' Merton was all concern. 'Then since you press me I shall accept with pleasure. It will be an honour.'

With great solicitude he accompanied them into the hotel, walking with them until they reached the Viscount's rooms.

'Until this evening...' With a beaming smile and a wave of his hand he left them.

'Edward, this is not wise.' Georgiana was frantic with terror. 'You should rest. He...Merton...was right. A blow to the head can be dangerous. Let us send word to cancel your invitation. He will understand. Perhaps another day...?'

Lyndhurst had not released his grip upon her arm, and now he drew her close. 'I can only thank those ruffians,' he said softly. 'Can it be that you do care after all?'

'Oh, no!' Georgiana struggled to free herself. 'I mean, of course, I care that you were hurt, as I would with anyone.'

'Anyone, my dearest?' He bent his head to hers, seeking her lips.

'Edward, you must not.' She turned her face away. 'You must be sensible.'

'I don't feel sensible at this moment. Georgiana, my darling, your face gives you away. Will you tell me that you do not love me?'

She could not look at him. Then a lean hand reached out to cup her chin. His lips found hers, and she was swept away on a dizzy tide of love and longing. When at last he released her she was breathless.

'That was not fair,' she protested.

'You have heard the old saying that all is fair in love and war?' He was laughing with pleasure as he looked at her.

'Please... My lord, do you not find something strange about the man who came to our aid?' Georgiana hung on to the last remnants of sanity. 'How did he come to be so close? His coach was waiting in the street.'

'Possibly he had an appointment there.' A cool finger traced the outlined of her lips. 'It was lucky for us...but put it out of your mind, my love.' He rested his face against her hair. 'These last days have been torture, Georgiana. I feared that I had lost you.'

'My lord—'

'Edward, I beg of you…'

'Well, then, Edward, please listen. We know nothing of this man. He could be as great a villain as those who attacked you. We cannot make a friend of him.'

'My dearest, you are overwrought. Your imagination is running away with you. This morning has been a shock, but you must not look for danger everywhere. Merton is an Englishman, of personable address, and you will admit that without his aid we should have been in poor case.'

'I know it, but…but he may have motives other than he claims.'

'Perhaps he plans to abduct you.' Lyndhurst's eyes twinkled. 'I should not blame him for the thought, but I suspect that you would make me jealous.'

'With that creature?' She shuddered. 'I would as soon seek the friendship of an adder.'

She had said too much. She knew it even as she spoke. Lyndhurst frowned, and she was uncomfortably aware of those clear, considering blue eyes intent upon her face.

'What is it?' he asked quietly. 'Have you met this man before?'

'No.' It was a reluctant reply. 'At least…only

briefly. He spoke to me in Calais, at the hotel. It was just to tell me where you were. I was looking for you, you see.'

'He did not insult you, I trust.'

'Of course not. He was all courtesy, but, Edward, I cannot trust him.'

'He should not have spoken to you without an introduction, Georgiana, but I cannot understand why you have taken him in such dislike.'

'Call it a woman's instinct…anything you like,' she cried wildly. 'He was at Dessein's. Now he is staying here at the Belle Ile. Does it not occur to you that he may have followed us?'

'For what purpose, my dear?' Lyndhurst gathered her gently into his arms. 'Most English travellers stay in certain recommended hotels. We might travel across Europe and see the same faces. It is no cause for alarm.'

Georgiana was silent. It was too late to explain. She should have told him of Merton's involvement with Harry and Richard long before this. Now both he and they were in danger. And she could not no longer delude herself. She would go to any lengths to keep Edward safe. A spasm of anguish crossed her face as she recalled the upraised cudgels and the ferocity of the men who had attacked him.

'I cannot bear to see you so distraught, my dearest love.'

'I thought…I thought they had killed you.' She hid her face in his coat.

'I am not so easily disposed of. Unprincipled brutes are difficult to murder.' He was teasing her, hoping to chase away the horror in her eyes. 'Besides, you threatened me with worse. I am scarred for life with the wounds that you inflicted.'

'I am sorry that I hurt you so.'

'The punishment was well deserved.' He took her hand and pressed his lips against her palm. Then he kissed each finger in turn. His mouth moved slowly to rest on the inside of her wrist, and travelled with delicious warmth along her bare arm.

'Please…!' she protested. 'I do not desire…'

'What do you desire? This…and this?' Lyndhurst nuzzled her neck. She jumped as his lips came to rest against the soft swell of her breasts.

In confusion she tugged at the low neckline of her gown, but her hands were held in a firm grip.

'I love you, Georgiana. You must not be afraid of me. In the words of the marriage service, I shall worship you with my body. When you become my wife you will understand that passion can be tender as well as wild.'

Despair threatened to overwhelm her. She could never be his wife, but the sweetness of his caresses tore her heart apart. She could not trust herself to speak.

Lyndhurst hesitated, and his voice was sad as he continued. 'I can only blame myself for your reluctance. When I came to your room the other night I behaved like a lout. Now you cannot bear my touch, and I don't blame you. I frightened you so badly.'

'No!' With an involuntary gesture she reached out to him. 'I am tired and confused, that is all. Will you give me time to compose myself?'

'All the time in the world.' His face lightened. 'And Georgiana, if you really do not wish to dine with Merton I will send a message.'

'It is of no consequence. Let us leave matters as they are.'

She had accepted the inevitable. Much as she disliked the thought of meeting Merton again, she must confront her enemy. It was better to learn something of his plans, if possible, than to continue in this fog of ignorance. Merton was cunning and sharp-witted, but wine might loosen his tongue. With some knowledge of his intentions she would find a way to save both Edward and her brother.

'It will be only for an hour or two,' Lyndhurst assured her. 'But we owe the man a certain courtesy for his help. I promise that he won't outstay his welcome. I shall plead my aching head...'

Georgiana gave him an anxious look. 'Is it very bad?'

'Certainly not, but the excuse will serve, if necessary. If you do not care to join us I'll explain that the shock has been too much for you.'

'I too owe him something,' she replied in a determined tone. 'I would not have him think me faint-hearted.'

'Never that!' Lyndhurst dropped a light kiss upon her brow. 'You are a veritable Amazon.' He was smiling as she left him.

She dressed with extra care that evening, and not only for her own satisfaction. Merton should be made to see that he was not dealing with some timid girl whom he could terrorise into obedience.

'It's pressed up lovely, miss.' Reverently, Betsy laid Georgiana's gown upon the bed. 'My uncle says that there's naught to bet French style for the ladies.'

Georgiana nodded as she slipped into the satin undergown. 'It was a ridiculous garment to pack,' she said ruefully. 'But we left London in haste, and I took the nearest things to hand.'

'Miss, I'm glad you did.' With deft fingers Betsy drew the gauze overdress about her mistress's shoulders. 'All the embroidery…' She shook her head in wonder at the tiny gold stars scattered at random on the flimsy fabric. 'Don't it look well against the white? Why, miss, you look just like a princess.'

Georgiana looked at her reflection in the mirror. The simple column of white satin made her look taller, and gave her an air of dignity, whilst the overdress softened the outlines of her figure. It would do very well for the purpose she had in mind.

She stood in silence as Betsy fastened the gold ribbon beneath her breasts. Then her glance travelled upwards. The last rays of the setting sun were streaming through the window behind her, turning her burnished curls into a flaming halo, but her eyes were steady. As green as the finest jade, they looked back at her, slanting and enormous, but without a trace of fear.

It was strange, but the thought of the ordeal ahead had served to restore her courage. Had she not heard somewhere that the best form of defence was attack? Tonight she would put that saying to the test.

She picked up her scarf and her fan and walked through into the parlour.

Both men rose as she entered the room. Then Lyndhurst walked towards her, his glowing look a tribute to her beauty. He kissed her hand, and the pressure of his fingers claimed her as his own.

'A vision indeed, madam!' Merton confined his greeting to the deepest of bows. 'We are honoured tonight by the company of the most enchanting woman in Paris.'

Georgiana returned the compliment with a slight curtsy. She kept her eyes demurely upon the ground, else her dagger-like look must surely have given her away. It cost her much to murmur some pleasantry in reply, but she would play her part in this charade. Tonight her acting abilities would be tested to the full.

In silence she allowed Lyndhurst to seat her at the table. Then she gave Merton her most ravishing smile.

'How fortunate we were that you happened by this morning in such an opportune way.'

'I beg that you will not speak of it.' Merton waved a dismissive hand. 'These incidents happen. They are best forgotten.'

'They are not easy to forget,' she said carefully. 'One should, perhaps, take them as a warning to be more careful in future.'

'How wise you are.' The silver eyes gazed into hers with meaning. 'I understand your concern, of course. His lordship might have been seriously injured.'

'As you say, the matter is best forgotten.' Lyndhurst's expression was pleasant enough, but there was a slight trace of impatience in his tone. He changed the subject.

'Do you stay long in Paris, sir?'

'A few days only, alas! When my business is concluded here I shall move on…perhaps to Brussels.'

'I have not been there since Waterloo. What a time that was! You will recall that our victory was a close-run thing.'

'Indeed! Had it not been for Blücher's timely arrival on the field we might have lost the day.'

Georgiana paid little attention to their discussion of military tactics. Brussels, she now knew with certainty, was not Merton's intended destination, but that information was of little help. Surreptitiously she signalled to the waiter to refill the gentlemen's glasses.

'We shall bore madam with our dull talk!' Merton exclaimed at last. 'The ladies do not care to think of death and danger.'

He had drunk deep, but the pock-marked face

showed no sign of it. Georgiana looked at the claw-like hand which curved around his glass. The finger-nails were clean and beautifully manicured, but he was older than she had first imagined. Dark brown age-spots showed up clearly against the taut skin.

'I believe we face what must be faced,' she told him quietly.

'With feminine resignation, I have no doubt.' His smile held no amusement. 'On occasion we must accept the inevitable.'

Lyndhurst's eyes roved from one face to the other, and as if aware of his regard Merton turned to his host.

'Madam is a philosopher, I see,' he remarked smoothly. 'She is a worthy antagonist.'

'You may be sure of it.' Lyndhurst laughed aloud. 'You will take a little more wine?'

Merton accepted, and Georgiana sighed with relief. She must be more careful. Edward had been quick to sense the tension in the room. It would not do to alert him further.

'This dish is so very good.' Merton tasted his *fricassée de poulets à l'italienne* with the air of a connoisseur. 'A transformation of the humble chicken! I compliment you upon your choice of menu, madam.'

'The compliments are due surely to the chef.' Georgiana had recovered her composure, and her words, if not warm, were at least civil. She entered as best she could into a discussion of French cooking and the wondrous flavours which resulted from the use of the freshest of ingredients. Yet there were undercurrents beneath the apparently innocuous remarks, and her uneasiness persisted.

Here, in their private room with her love beside her and the servants close at hand, it was folly to imagine that harm might come either to herself or Edward, but Merton's brooding presence cast a pall upon her spirit.

Apparently at ease, he lolled back in his chair, twirling the stem of the wine glass between his fingers.

She was not deceived. He was waiting…waiting…but for what?

She was not long in doubt. When Scroggins appeared with a murmured message Lyndhurst rose to his feet.

'Will you forgive me if I leave you for a moment? There is some trifling matter which will not wait. A fellow below claims to have found my snuff-box. I must have lost it in the struggle.'

His loving look was intended to reassure Georgiana, but her nerves were on edge. This was some trick, she was convinced. She made as if to rise, but Lyndhurst's hand pressed gently upon her shoulder.

'You will entertain our guest for a short time?'

She swallowed and nodded, but inside she felt that she was screaming silently. There was an aura of evil about Merton. Why could not Edward see it? With widened eyes she fought a rising ride of panic as she looked at the man across the table.

He waited until the door had closed upon his host before he spoke.

'A mere stratagem, my dear. You guessed, of course?' He did not wait for her reply. 'We must talk, Miss Westleigh. You are aware of your brother's position, I believe?'

'I know that you have used him for your own ends.'

'Oh, come…we are not speaking of children. Both young men were ready enough to grasp the opportunity of gain. An expensive lifestyle has its charms, especially in London, but pleasure must be paid for, as they came to realise.'

'With robbery? That they did not know.'

'An ugly word, Miss Westleigh, but I see that you are a realist, and we are wasting time. Your brother has told you of my plans. Believe me when I tell you that you have no choice but to agree with them.'

As he bent towards her she was reminded of some great predatory bird, hovering for the kill. Beneath the hooked nose his mouth was thin and cruel, and those strange eyes seemed to bore into the furthest recesses of her mind.

'There is always a choice,' she said coldly. 'As yet, the Viscount knows nothing of your involvement with his brother. Suppose I were to tell him?'

'You will not, I think. This morning's attack was intended to convince you that I have it within my power to kill him. I should not hesitate to do so…and that, my dear, you would not wish.'

'He is nothing to me,' she lied.

'No?' He gave a laugh of pure enjoyment. 'One has only to see you together to know that your regard for him is equal to his for you.'

When she did not reply he spoke again.

'Are you wondering why I saved him? It was for the best of reasons. Fear for his life will guarantee your compliance with my wishes.'

'And they are?'

'That you accompany your brother and his friend to a destination of my choice. There you will work for me.'

'You do not allow for the Viscount's vigilance. Escape is not as easy as you would have me believe.'

'Ah, you are thinking of that bungled first attempt. It was a mistake on my part to listen to your brother. One should not send a boy on a man's errand. Next time I shall handle matters myself.'

'Next time?' she breathed.

'Not quite yet. You may enjoy a few more days with your handsome lover. There are certain arrangements to be made. I intend to leave nothing to chance.'

'What a loathsome creature you are!' Georgiana was breathing fast. 'You may rest assured that I shall do all in my power to destroy you.'

'But, my dear, you have no power of any kind. Now let us have done with this childish nonsense. When I send for you, you will do as you are bidden.' Merton looked up with a smile as Lyndhurst returned to join them.

'Success, my lord? Your property is returned?'

'Surprising, is it not?' The Viscount held up the missing snuff-box. 'The fellow traced me by the crest. An honest rogue! He might have sold it for a few francs.'

'I am sure that he did not lose by his honesty.'

Merton examined the fine workmanship of the precious object. 'Now, my lord, I must beg you to excuse me, with my thanks for a most enjoyable evening. Miss Westleigh has been so gracious...'

Again, he did not attempt to take her hand as he made his farewells, but his bow was low. 'I bid you *au revoir*, rather than goodbye, in the hope that we shall meet again.'

Conscious of Lyndhurst's eyes upon her, she inclined her head. Then, her back rigid, she turned away.

'That was something of a trial for you, I fear.' Lyndhurst took her in his arms as the door closed. 'Merton is a strange creature. We need not see more of him, but we have done our duty.' He dropped a gentle kiss upon her brow. 'I am sorry to have left you alone with him.'

'It did not matter.' Her voice was colourless and he looked at her intently.

'You are very tired, my dearest. I should not have pressed you to join us. The day has been long...'

'And full of incident.' She managed the ghost of a smile though her heart was breaking. 'Oh, Edward, I was so afraid for you...'

'Set your mind at rest. It is over, though I'll admit I shouldn't care to repeat the experience.'

'Next time you will carry a pistol. Will you promise me as much?'

'Of course!' He bent his head and found her lips.

Georgiana clung to him with a passion that matched his own. In a few days' time they would be parted forever. If this was to be their final chance of happiness she would not deny him anything he asked.

'My love!' His hands slid down her arms, drawing her close until their bodies were as one. 'What a temptress you are!' His voice was thick with passion. 'You had best go, else I shall forget my resolution.'

'I wish you would.' She hid her face in his coat.

'What did you say?' He tilted her chin until he could look into her eyes. 'Georgiana, are you sure?'

'Quite sure.' She was blushing, but her voice was steady. 'Edward, I love you dearly. I ask only that we share our love.'

He picked her up then and carried her through into his room. With reverent hands he stroked her hair.

'Let us be married tomorrow,' he said quietly. 'My darling wife, I promise to make you happy.'

His words were bittersweet, and her eyes filled with tears.

'No... This is too sweet a moment for sorrow.

Kiss me, my love!' His mouth closed on hers, gentle but insistent, and her response was immediate. As the soft flesh met her own she gave a cry, and her arms closed about his neck.

Then she was aware of a firm hand cupping her breast, the thumb caressing her nipple through the thin fabric of her gown. She made an inarticulate sound as she felt it harden. Only half-aware of the gauze overdress being slipped from her shoulders, she made no protest as the satin undergarment whispered to the ground.

'Let me look at you.' Lyndhurst held her away from him, his eyes feasting upon her loveliness.

Quite naked, she faced him proudly, secure in the knowledge of her own beauty. Her shyness had left her. Now she was all woman, waiting for the consummation which would bind her forever to her lover.

Murmuring endearments, Lyndhurst laid her upon the bed. She watched quietly as he removed his coat, his shirt and his breeches.

In the candlelight his torso gleamed, highlighting the heavily muscled back and thighs. Perfectly proportioned, his wide shoulders narrowed to a trim waist, and below it his stomach was as flat as that of any athlete. Embarrassed by his arousal, she turned to blow out the last of the candles, but he stayed her with a loving look.

'We have no need of darkness, dearest heart. I want to see your face as you love me. You cannot know how I have longed for you...to see those wondrous eyes fill with desire, and to know that you are mine...'

He tossed away the coverlet and lay beside her, caressing, teasing and stroking until she yearned for fulfilment. When it came she cried out in pain, but it was a precious agony.

Then she was swept away on a tide of passion, her rhythmic movements keeping pace with his until she felt a strange sensation. The tingling began in her toes and consumed her body until it ended in the centre of her being. Fierce cries escaped her lips until the spasmodic pulsing eased.

'Edward...my love!' Spent and exhausted, she drew the dark head to her breast.

'My darling, you are a jewel! To think how I misjudged you!' A teasing note crept into his voice. 'I feared you would shrink from my very touch.'

'But I did not.' Feminine and sure of him, she was triumphant.

'No, you did not. I don't deserve such happiness.' He settled her into the crook of his arm. 'To think that we have a lifetime ahead of us…'

His words brought Georgiana back to reality and she stiffened.

'What is it, my love?' His gentle hands began to stroke her. 'Misgivings? Do you regret…?'

'No!' It was almost a cry of protest. 'I regret nothing. But, Edward, we cannot marry yet.'

'Why not?' His teeth nipped tenderly at her ear. 'You could be pregnant, Georgiana. If passion is the key, then there can be no doubt of it.'

He was laughing as he spoke, and was unprepared for her reaction. The colour drained from her face as she freed herself from his embrace.

'No, no! That cannot be,' she whispered.

'It would be but natural.'

She heard the surprise and the hurt in his voice, but she was silent. To have a child when she must leave him? What a fool she had been! When she had offered him her love she had been heedless of the possible consequences.

'You must not fear childbirth, Georgiana.' Long fingers traced the outline of her spine. 'It can be dangerous, I know, but you would have the best of care. Nothing shall happen to my wife.'

'Edward, I do not fear it,' she said earnestly.

'Nothing would please me more than to give you a son...'

'Or a daughter...but you are my main consideration.' He was looking down at her with the smile she loved so well.

'Even so...' she faltered. 'We should wait. We have not yet resolved...'

'You believe that your brother might object? He has little cause to do so.' Edward slipped out of bed and put on his robe. 'You owe him nothing, Georgiana. He is not your keeper, rather the reverse. He must learn to stand on his own feet.'

'I know, and I have told him so, but may we not tell him before we...before we take this step?'

'We must find him first.' Lyndhurst's voice was ironic. 'Dear Harry...I am beginning to dislike the very sound of his name.'

'You do not know him.' Georgiana hung her head. 'And he is dear to me.'

'I need no convincing of that fact.' Lyndhurst's scowl was replaced by a smile. 'You are loyal, my Venus, but I warn you...when we are married Harry's welfare shall not come before your own.'

Her ready agreement appeared to satisfy him, but it was with a heavy heart that she left him to seek her own room.

Chapter Nine

Georgiana's sorrow could not last. It was banished by the memory of the hours she had spent in her lover's embrace. How sweet it had been to know him fully. Her lips curved in a reminiscent smile as she thought of the old biblical expression. In the past she had considered it a curious phrase, but now she knew its meaning.

She felt bruised and sore, though Edward had been the soul of tenderness. And it had been worth that first sharp pang of agony to soar with him into a world of unimaginable joy.

She would not give him up, if it meant killing Merton herself. That creature would not steal away her happiness, nor harm her loved ones. She had given herself to Edward almost in despair, fearing that she must part from him forever, but the love they had shared had strengthened her courage. Now she would fight Merton with every means at her command. Nothing would stand in her way.

How thin was the veneer of civilisation, she thought ruefully. Were not women supposed to be the gentle sex? Yet the thoughts which filled her mind were far from gentle. She felt like a tigress in defence of her young. Given the opportunity she would destroy her enemy without compunction.

With that comforting prospect in mind, she fell asleep.

It was late morning when she awoke to find Betsy standing by her bed.

'Oh, miss, did I waken you? His lordship said as how you was not to be disturbed... I came in to see if you needed anything.'

'My breakfast...and then hot water.' Georgiana stretched luxuriously. She had never felt more fully alive, and she could not wait to see Edward. 'His lordship has breakfasted already?'

Betsy chuckled. 'He was up betimes. He's been gone out these three hours...'

'Gone where?' Georgiana was puzzled. Edward had said nothing of an appointment.

'I don't know, miss.' Betsy looked at Georgiana's troubled face. 'There's nothing amiss,' she comforted. 'My uncle said as how he'd never seen the master look so cheerful. He promised to be back by noon.'

'Then I had best hurry.' She swallowed the scalding coffee, and nibbled at a croissant. 'Have I anything fit to wear?'

She looked with distaste at the primrose-yellow gown which Betsy had laid across a chair. Careful pressing could not disguise the fact that the fabric was looking tired.

'I should have brought more clothes,' she murmured. Somehow it seemed important that she should look her best for Edward on that particular morning.

'This came for you.' Betsy laid a large green box upon the bed. Her eyes were sparkling as they pleaded with Georgiana to open it without delay.

'For me?'

'Yes, miss. My uncle knows the name…it's famous. And…and I was to give you this.' She produced a small flat parcel from her pocket.

'From whom?' Georgiana asked in surprise.

'It's from his lordship.' With unabashed curiosity Betsy craned her neck to examine the contents of the package. It contained a leather jewel-box.

'Oh! How beautiful!' Georgiana gasped as she looked at a string of perfectly matched pearls which nestled against the velvet lining. Beside them lay a note bearing the simple message 'For my love'. It bore no signature, and none was needed.

'Will you wear it today, miss?' Betsy's eyes were round as she looked at the necklace. 'Pearls takes their glow from a lady's skin, so my uncle says.'

'Yes... Fasten it for me, will you?' Georgiana allowed the milky string to slide through her fingers before she opened the diamond clasp. 'I must take care not to lose it.'

'That you must. But, miss, the other box...?'

With eager fingers Georgiana tore at the wrapping. The box contained a charming gown of snow-white cambric trimmed with palest blue ribbon. Tiny knots adorned the bodice and the flounced hem, and edged the short, puffed sleeves, yet the effect was one of simplicity.

'It will match your chipstraw bonnet,' Betsy cried happily. 'You'll look so fine, Miss Georgiana, and it's such a lovely day. You won't need your cloak.'

'I wasn't planning to go out,' Georgiana said, but she could not resist the temptation to wear her new gown.

She looked at her reflection in the glass. Today her face was vivid, and her skin had a special glow. Her jade-green eyes laughed back at her as if they held some secret known only to herself.

Edward's expression mirrored her mood as he greeted her in the parlour. A brown hand reached up to stroke her hair.

'You are lovelier than ever,' he murmured. 'My darling, I still can't believe that you love me.'

'But you must.' She laughed up at him. 'Look into my eyes! Can you be in any doubt?'

A kiss was her reply, and it took her breath away. Again she was borne on that dizzying tide of rapture as she clung to him. Then he held her at arm's length, and shook her gently.

'Temptress!' he said gaily. 'You shall not divert me from my purpose. Come, my dearest, I have a surprise for you.' He took her hand and was about to lead her from the room.

'Edward, I have not thanked you…' Georgiana's hand went to the pearls about her neck. 'These are so beautiful. I shall treasure them all my life.'

'But not as much as I shall treasure you…' He

bent to kiss her again, but, laughing, she averted her head.

'And my gown… Will you not let me thank you?'

'The way you look is thanks enough. Georgiana, my darling, I would give you everything…'

'There is no need. You have given me yourself. That is all I ask or need.' She lifted her face to his and his mouth came down on hers.

Once more she was lost to everything about her as she responded to the insistent pressure of his lips. With an inarticulate murmur she reached up to throw her arms about his neck, holding him close as she caressed his hair.

'I love you so,' she whispered.

'Witch! You will drive me mad with desire. Let us go, or I won't be responsible for my actions…'

Georgiana could not mistake the look of longing in his eyes and she blushed a little.

'Still shy?' he teased. 'After last night I thought…'

She laid a soft hand over his lips, but she was laughing as she replied. 'My lord, you shall not put me out of countenance.'

'Not yet, perhaps, but tonight…' His fingers wandered the full length of her spine, and it tingled in happy anticipation. 'Tonight, my love, we shall learn more about each other… The bond between us will grow and strengthen, now that we are one flesh.'

'I know it.' She looked at him with perfect trust. 'Edward, I am so happy.'

'And I.' With a loving smile he took her arm. 'My dearest, we must go.'

'But where?'

'That I shall not tell you. It is to be a surprise.'

'A pleasant one?'

'I trust you will think so. The drive to our destination is not far.'

Dreamy-eyed and languorous, Georgiana paid little attention to her surroundings as the carriage bowled through the narrow streets of the French capital. The man beside her occupied her mind to the exclusion of all else.

She was intensely aware of his physical presence, smiling as she thought of the sheer athletic perfection of that powerful frame. As always, his dress was immaculate, if unobtrusive in its elegance. It was no wonder that his striking figure drew all eyes, but she alone could compare him to the Apollo of the Belvedere.

Last night she had seen the wonder of her lover

as nature made him. She had covered the lean, hard body with kisses, stroking the heavily muscled back and thighs, whilst wondering at the smoothness of his tanned skin. The faint male scent of him had excited her, even as he had aroused her with his caresses.

Her glance rested on his hands and her colour rose. Those long, graceful fingers had aroused her to unimaginable heights of passion, questing, exploring and teasing. Even now, as she looked at them, she felt a stirring of desire.

'Georgiana?' Edward was smiling down at her. Then he took her hand in his and pressed his lips against her palm. 'Still tired, my darling? I feel I used you roughly.'

Her blush deepened. 'I...I am not tired... But where are we going, Edward?'

'We are there.' He threw open the carriage door and swung to the ground. Then he reached up to help her down.

Georgiana looked about her in surprise. It was clear that they had reached the outskirts of the city, as green fields stretched on either side. No dwellings of any size lay before them, except for a hostelry and a church.

'What is this place?' she asked.

'It is the home of an old acquaintance.' Edward took her hand and led her along the pathway to the church. At the porch he turned aside and tapped on the door of an adjoining building.

It was opened by a tubby man with twinkling eyes. His tonsure proclaimed his calling.

'Come in, my son.' The priest stood aside to allow his guests to precede him. Then he followed them into a small study.

Georgiana looked at him with interest. His expression was genial, but his bright blue eyes were shrewd as he gazed at her. Then he turned to her companion.

'You wish the ceremony to take place at once, my lord?'

'If Georgiana agrees. My dearest, will you marry me today? I know you have been troubled, but as my wife no harm will come to you…'

Georgiana's mind was in a whirl. This, then, was the reason for the white gown, the pearls…?

'My lord, you should have told me of your plans,' she demurred.

'Would you have agreed?'

She was silent. Suddenly her fears returned. If Merton should discover her marriage he might go to any lengths…

She looked at Edward and his expression broke her heart. In his eyes doubt was mingled with apprehension. On an impulse she reached out to him.

'I wish for nothing more than to be your wife,' she assured him.

'My dearest, you are quite sure? I promised you time to consider but I cannot wait, and I feared that something…someone…might cause you to refuse me.'

His eyes searched her face, and for a moment her heart misgave her. There was so much she had not told him. He believed that her regard for Harry was the sole cause of her hesitation, but there was more…much more. If she agreed to wed him now she might be putting his own life at risk.

'I have overborne your wishes with this stratagem.' Edward clasped her hand with a rueful look. 'I wanted to carry you off…to still your doubts here, in this church. Was I wrong to try to persuade you, Georgiana?'

'No, my love.' She made up her mind on the instant. 'If the good father will marry us I am happy to agree.'

Edward's glowing look was enough to fill her heart with joy. Her doubts vanished like snow in summer, and with a beating heart she allowed him to lead her through into the simple church. When they were married she would tell him everything.

She looked up at the tall, straight figure standing beside her at the altar. He had all her heart and all her trust. How foolish she had been to try to carry her burdens alone. Edward would cherish her and protect her, and she had faith in his judgement.

The ceremony was brief, but as her lover pledged his troth to her she treasured every word. Her own replies were made in a low voice, but they came from her heart. Never before had she understood the full beauty of the marriage service. The vows she made that day she would keep forever.

Those sacred moments ended when Edward kissed her. Then he raised her hand to his lips, saluting her wedding ring.

'May I offer my good wishes for your happiness, Viscountess Lyndhurst?' The tubby little parish priest was beaming with pleasure. 'I have no doubt of it myself. Your husband is a worthy man.'

With many congratulations he ushered them back to the carriage, and waved until they were out of sight.

Edward slipped an arm about Georgiana's waist and drew her close. 'Well, my dear wife, was the ordeal very dreadful?'

'Oh, Edward, it was beautiful! I thought I must disgrace you by bursting into tears of happiness.'

'Dear love!' His kiss was very gentle. 'I had not thought to know such joy. How good you are! It would have served me well if you had refused me out of pique.'

'What can you mean?' Her eyes were very bright.

'I did abduct you,' he teased. 'At least, I did not tell you of my plans. Have you forgiven me the deception?'

'Certainly not! You must know, my lord, that a long betrothal is considered proper.'

'How long?' He buried his face in her neck.

'At least, at the very least, two years.' She kept her eyes demurely on her lap.

'It couldn't be done,' he announced solemnly. 'Why, you will have given me two babes by then…' He kissed her again as she began to blush. 'What a delight you are! A creature of fire and snow! I could not have guessed that my love would be returned in such good part.'

'But you know it now,' she whispered.

'Yes, I know it now. What a life we shall have together, my darling! It will be my pleasure to give you everything your heart can desire. When we return to England we shall go first to Lyndhurst. Then, if you wish it, we may return to Europe, or visit the Indies, if you prefer.'

Georgiana listened in a daze of happiness as he told her of his home, and his estates abroad. Now he would be by her side forever, yet only that morning her future had promised to be bleak in the extreme. These last few hours had transformed her life in a way for which she had not dared to hope.

For the rest of that day the hours flew by. Lyndhurst dismissed the hotel servants, and they were attended only by a smiling Betsy and her uncle.

On being informed of his master's good fortune, Scroggins said all that was proper on the occasion, but his attitude to Georgiana was unbending. He addressed her correctly, but her title seemed to stick in his throat.

'Give him time,' Edward said cheerfully. 'He's a dry stick, but he has a good heart.'

Georgiana sighed to herself. Privately she wondered if Scroggins would ever accept her. Doubtless he thought her an adventuress, who had trapped his master into marriage. Loyalty was all very well in its way, she mused, but in this case she sensed suspicion and hostility.

News of the Viscount's marriage swept the

hotel, and that evening it was clear that the chef had outdone himself. A feast awaited them, but excitement prevented Georgiana from doing justice to the meal. She ate when pressed to do so, but she could not have named the dishes.

Her eyes were on her lover's face, caressing, even in her thoughts, that beautifully curved mouth and the clean lines of his profile. He sensed her regard, and reached across the table to press her hand.

'I could eat you rather than this.' He laughed as he waved a dismissive hand at the viands on the table. 'Have I told you how beautiful you are?'

'You mentioned it,' she teased.

He came round to sit beside her, cupping her face in a firm grip.

'Possibly I did not say that those wonderful eyes remind me of the summer sea, deep green and fathomless.'

'But, my lord, you tell me that you are able always to fathom my innermost thoughts…'

'Not always, Georgiana…' His face grew serious. 'Sometimes I wonder…'

Now, if ever, was the time to speak, the time to unburden herself of the full story of Merton, and his hold upon Harry, but she could not bring herself to do it.

Tonight she would not ruin Edward's happiness. Tomorrow would be time enough to embroil him in the sorry mess of her brother's affairs. Perhaps it was weak of her to put off the moment when she must tell him the full story, but this was her wedding day, and it was precious to her.

'You cannot wonder at my love,' she said gently.

'I shall wonder at it all my life. My dearest wife, I want you so much…'

'And I you, Edward…'

With a muttered exclamation he swept her into his arms and carried her to her room.

His hands were gentle as he untied the ribbon beneath her breasts. Then he drew the flimsy cambric gown over her head and laid it aside. His kisses were urgent as he removed her undergarments. Then he held her away from him, his eyes feasting on her beauty.

'You drive me mad with desire,' he whispered as he bent his head to her naked breasts. 'Tonight, my darling, I will show you what love truly means.'

He threw back the coverlet and laid her on the bed. His coat was quickly thrown aside, but as he began to unbutton his shirt the door burst open.

'Harry!' Georgiana clutched at the coverlet to

hide her naked body as her brother stormed into the room. His face was ashen, but there was murder in his eyes. With a cry of rage he launched himself at Lyndhurst.

Edward sidestepped the sudden charge with ease. As Harry turned, reaching for his throat, he caught the younger man's wrists in an iron grip, forcing him to his knees.

'How dare you burst into your sister's room without a by-your-leave?' he demanded. 'Have you no respect for her privacy?'

'Respect?' It was a shout of rage. 'She deserves none, and nor do you. I'll kill you for this!'

'Be quiet!' the Viscount thundered. 'Another insult to my wife and I'll thrash you within an inch of your life.'

'Your wife?' The fight went out of Harry as he stared at Lyndhurst. 'I…I don't believe you,' he muttered. 'This is some trick. It won't be the first time, will it, my lord?'

Lyndhurst struck him across the mouth. 'You young puppy! I am minded to thrash you anyway.'

'To stop me from speaking the truth? Does my sister know how you dishonoured the woman to whom you were betrothed, and then abandoned her?'

'So you listen to gossip, do you?' Edward released his grip and allowed Edward to rise to his feet. 'That accusation is beneath contempt. I shall not trouble to answer it.'

'Because you can't.' Harry stood very straight and still as he turned to his sister. 'Georgie, come with me now. You can't stay here. I don't care what you have done...'

'That is generous of you, Harry.' Georgiana was furious with him, and her voice was dangerously quiet. 'I have done nothing of which I need be ashamed. Edward is telling the truth. We were married in church this morning.'

'Doubtless by some friend of his, dressed as a parson.' Harry's handsome face was an ugly mask of bitterness. 'He has deceived you for his own ends.' He gasped in pain as steely fingers gripped his arm.

'You will withdraw that remark.' Lyndhurst's eyes glittered with anger.

'I will not withdraw. Name your seconds, sir. I will meet you at a place of your choosing.'

'Stop it!' Georgiana stared at him. 'Harry, you are behaving like an idiot. I am Edward's wife— his *wife,* do you understand? You may believe it or not, as you choose, but nothing will alter the fact that we are married.'

Her words held utter conviction, and Harry made a gesture of despair.

'How could you, Georgie? To go behind my back... I had not thought it of you. You might have warned me...'

'You were always by my side, of course.' She could not resist the taunt.

'I know... I should not have left you. I am to blame for all of this.' He hung his head.

'Oh, Hal!' Georgiana threw up her hands in exasperation. 'How little you know me! Do you think I would marry for any reason other than love?'

'You can't love Lyndhurst,' he said sulkily.

'But I do.' She bestowed a tender glance on Edward and he came to her at once, taking her hand and dropping a kiss upon her fingers.

'He's a monster,' Harry announced. The freckles which stood out against his pale skin served to give him the appearance of a disappointed child.

Lyndhurst's shout of laughter surprised both Georgiana and her brother. He held out a hand to Harry.

'Let us be friends,' he said. 'I do not blame you for your anger. You wished only to defend Georgiana's honour, but she is now in my care.

For her sake, if for no other reason, we must not quarrel. Her happiness will always be my first concern.'

'And Edward is not a monster,' Georgiana said proudly. She gazed into her husband's eyes and Harry could not mistake that look of love.

'Then I suppose I must wish you happy.' His manner was stiff. He did not intend to be mollified too easily.

'Will you give me a kiss?' Georgiana was radiant. 'Harry, I am well content.'

'I am glad of it.' His carefree manner returned as he saluted her, disarmed by her evident joy. 'What a think to happen! Richard won't believe it—!' He stopped and shot an uneasy glance at Lyndhurst.

'Harry, where is my brother?' The Viscount's voice was calm. 'I should like to see him.'

'He isn't far away.' Harry shifted from one foot to the other as he debated with himself. Then he reached a decision. 'I'll take you to him if you wish.'

'At once, if you please!'

'Edward, won't it wait until tomorrow?' Suddenly Georgiana was uneasy. She should have told him of Merton's involvement with the two young men. Now he would learn the story from their own lips. She had no doubt that he would insist on the whole truth. Then he would realise that she had not been frank with him.

'I shall not be long away from you, my dearest.' He blew her a kiss as he accompanied Harry from the room.

She waited for what seemed like hours, until at last she fell asleep, her lips curved in a tender smile. At last it did not matter that Edward had found the fugitives. He had been kind to Harry, in spite of her brother's reluctance to accept his friendship. Now all their problems were in his hands, and he would know what to do.

She stirred as a noise awakened her. Then she sat bolt upright. In the light of a single candle a figure moved towards her.

'Edward?' she murmured.

'Were you expecting someone else? Merton, perhaps…?' Edward's voice was raw with anger.

She could see only the faint outline of his face. Then he held the candle high, and she gave a cry of horror. She was looking into the eyes of a stranger. That mask-like countenance bore no resemblance to the man she loved so well, and she shrivelled at his expression of revulsion.

'You need not shrink from me,' the cynical

voice continued. 'I would not touch you if you were the last woman alive.'

'Edward, please...' Georgiana held out her arms in supplication. 'Only let me explain... I meant to tell you what had happened, but there was no opportunity.'

'No? You lay in my arms...you told me you loved me...whilst you laughed behind my back. When I think of that evening with Merton! How you must both have enjoyed my ignorance of what was afoot!'

'So it is wounded pride which makes you treat me as an enemy...?' Georgiana shivered. She felt icy cold.

'Not pride, my dear, but a sense of betrayal. In my folly I had imagined that you trusted me, yet since we met I have never had your confidence.'

'That is not true, I—'

He silenced her with a look.

'Will you deny that you knew of Merton's villainy? That you have known since we were at Calais?'

'I don't deny it,' she said dully. 'But they told me you would be killed...'

'So your silence was the price of my life?' His laugh was filled with scorn. 'What kind of a man do you think me?'

Georgiana did not reply.

'Unlike your brother I do not care to hide behind your petticoats,' he continued. 'Is it true that you planned to go with Merton?'

'I… We had no choice. It was either your life or that of Harry and your brother.'

'I will take care of my own!' he said savagely. 'If you think so little of me, I wonder why you married me.'

'It was because I love you,' she cried in anguish.

'Love? You don't know the meaning of the word. Love is not simply passion, Georgiana. It demands faith and trust between husband and wife.'

'Like your faith and trust in me?' Georgiana's eyes filled.

'Spare me your tears. This time they will not serve to sway me. You speak of my trust in you?' His laugh was ugly. 'Was it to continue when you disappeared again? The vows you made this morning meant nothing, I suppose?'

'I meant every word of them,' she sobbed. 'I would not have left you, Edward; I had changed my mind. Tonight I meant to tell you all…'

'Another pack of lies and half-truths? Madam, you sicken me. Whether you go or stay is now a matter of indifference to me.'

'You are hateful,' she cried wildly. 'Go! Get out of my sight.'

'It will be a pleasure.' With an ironic bow he left her.

Chapter Ten

Georgiana had never felt so wretched in her life. She buried her head in her pillow and wept until she had no tears left. In a few short hours her world had tumbled about her ears, and on this, her wedding day…

It was so unfair. She had acted with the best of intentions in an effort to protect both Edward and Harry, but she had succeeded in doing neither.

Edward hated her. She would not soon forget the expression in his eyes. They had held contempt, disgust and, above all, anger. He was not a man to forgive or forget an insult to his honour. He would have his revenge, she was sure of it, and now Harry too was at his mercy.

To sleep was impossible. She rose and dressed

and began to pace the room. What on earth was she to do? To be tied for life to a man who loathed her was a fate beyond her worst nightmares, especially as she…as she…

Her lips quivered, then she straightened her shoulders. She did not love him. It was impossible. How could any woman care for someone who had treated her so cruelly? And he had been cruel. Harry was right. Edward was a monster. He had taken her love and flung it back in her face…

She sat by her window for hours until the first pale light of dawn streaked across the sky. Her cheeks were burning, but her hands were icy cold.

She had come to a decision in those lonely hours. She could not stay with Edward; that was clear. He must agree to annul their marriage.

The prospect brought her no comfort, but it was the only solution. She could not bear to see him every day…to be in his presence and to live with his contempt. He had found his brother; perhaps that would be enough to send him back to England.

If she could escape with Harry her husband would think himself well rid of her. Then she remembered Merton and her heart sank. Edward would not leave until he had settled his account with the man who had brought his brother to ruin;

she knew him well enough to know that. And it would be no affair of honour, to be settled between gentlemen. Merton was more likely to resort to a knife in the back.

She sank her head in her hands. It was all very well for Edward to claim that he could take care of himself, but was he prepared for treachery? He did not know Merton as she did.

Yet it was no concern of hers. She must steel herself against any softening towards him. She sat as if turned to stone, and did not turn her head as Betsy entered the room.

'I hope I did right, miss—I mean madam. With his lordship gone I thought you might be wanting your breakfast.'

Georgiana looked at her with brimming eyes. She could not speak.

'There, there, my lady... You must not take on so. Why, you look like a ghost this morning...' With scant regard for ceremony she threw a comforting arm about Georgiana's shoulders.

The presence of a friendly face was the undoing of her mistress. Georgiana began to sob.

'I'm sorry, Betsy. I don't mean to be so foolish.'

'A lovers' quarrel, is it, Miss Georgiana? Well, gentlemen is funny critturs. There's no understanding them.' Betsy's hug was bear-like. 'Leave 'em be, is what I say. They comes round in the end.'

'Betsy, you are wise beyond your years.' Georgiana smiled through her tears. 'But this time you are wrong.'

'Bless you, they're all the same. I ain't no beauty, but the village lads be strong for me…'

'I'm not surprised. Dear Betsy, how kind you are!'

'That's as may be,' came the sturdy reply. 'Now, madam, I was to tell you that his lordship will be back betimes. You are to wait for him in the parlour.'

'I see!' Georgiana was infuriated. How dared Edward send his instructions by the servants?

'My uncle says as how his lordship be on his high ropes this morning,' Betsy ventured.

'Then he may come down from them.' Georgiana was too angry to consider the wisdom of her words.

Betsy giggled, though she endeavoured to look solemn. 'Will you wear the white again?' she asked.

'Certainly not! The yellow will do well enough.'

Betsy was clever enough to hold her tongue. She dressed her mistress in silence.

It was several hours before Edward returned. Meantime Georgiana was a prey to conflicting emotions. Anger gave way to despair, and finally to the faint hope that he might have softened towards her.

One look at his face was enough to disabuse her of that idea. It was expressionless. He came towards her and bowed with formal courtesy. She might have been a stranger.

'I shall not keep you over-long,' he began. 'But there are certain matters to discuss. I intend to remain in Paris for some time. No doubt you will not wish to stay here. I you will tell me of your plans I will provide you with funds…'

'I want nothing from you,' she said coldly.

'You are still my wife, and my responsibility. What do you intend to do?'

'I…I have no plans.'

'You surprise me! That fertile mind must have at least a dozen schemes… Come, madam, we are wasting time. Let us reach an agreement quickly, then I'll relieve you of my company.'

'I shall not leave my brother.' Her eyes were defiant as she faced him squarely.

'I see. What an optimist you are! Neither you nor he will continue your association with Merton. You may be sure of that.'

'What do you mean to do?' Georgiana began to tremble. There was murder in his face.

'I intend to wait for his return. The bird has flown, possibly to attend to the "arrangements" of which he told you. As yet he does not know that I have found his victims.'

'He may not come back,' she breathed.

'He'll come back. Nothing is more certain. Are you not an essential part of his schemes?'

Georgiana did not argue. There was little point. He would not believe a word she said.

'I am concerned only for my brother,' she said. 'You have not told me…'

'He is unharmed. I shall honour his commitments, and those of Richard too.'

'We cannot accept…' Swift colour flooded Georgiana's face.

'Madam, you have no choice. This is my decision and your brother has agreed.'

She was on her feet in an instant. 'Oh, how could he?' she cried. 'He should have asked me first.'

'Still interfering, my dear? When will you learn that your brother is a man grown, if a foolish one? On this occasion he found it reasonable that I, as his brother-in-law, should offer my help. His gratitude was somewhat overwhelming.'

'Then…then he may return to England?'

'Not for the moment. He will go to India, as I suggested. You may, of course, accompany him if you wish, though I would not recommend the climate for a female. England would be a better choice for you. I will write to your father…'

'You will do no such thing!' She gave him a dagger-like look. 'I won't be packed off like some useless baggage.'

'A baggage, certainly,' he purred. 'But useless? Hardly. You are not in your best looks this morning, but that may soon be remedied.'

With a speed which caught her unawares he seized her in his arms.

'Let me go!' she cried. 'Last night you said that you had no wish to touch me.'

'I spoke in haste, my dear. After all, when a man is married he is entitled to expect some comfort from his wife.'

'You will get none from me!' Georgiana struggled in vain to break his grip. 'I hate you!'

'That need not diminish our pleasure, my dear.' His hand cupped her breast, and his thumb caressed her nipple gently.

Her response was instant and could not be denied. Furious in the knowledge that her body could betray her, she bent her head and sank her teeth into his wrist. Then she cried out in pain as he caught at her hair and forced her head back.

'Have you forgotten your marriage vows so soon?' he sneered. 'I seem to remember something about obedience.'

'I will never obey you,' she panted. 'I did not know you when I made those vows.'

'Nor I you, apparently.' He flung her away from him. 'Nevertheless, we are handfasted, and you will do your duty.'

'You…you are trying to frighten me,' she accused. 'If you think to drive me back to England with your threats you will not do it.'

'So it is to be India? As you wish, though I warn you, madam… You bear my name, and I will not have it dragged through the mud.'

'I have no intention of using it. I do not care to be associated with you, or any member of your family.'

'Especially as your own is beyond reproach.'

'That, my lord, is the cheapest of gibes,' Georgiana said with dignity. 'If you have done with me, I shall retire.'

'Oh, I have not done with you, my dear…far from it; but you may go. Incidentally, my brother dines with us this evening, and Harry too.'

Georgiana had reached the door, but his words stopped her. She looked up in surprise, but Edward had turned away and was gazing through the window. She left him without comment.

The evening promised to be a trial, but the reality was worse. Georgiana tried to smile as Richard kissed her shyly and wished her years of happiness. Harry, too, was in buoyant mood, toasting the bride again and again as he chaffed her and congratulated Edward.

Georgiana writhed inwardly. Neither of them could know that they were turning the knife in the wound. She stole a glance at Edward, wondering if he felt as she did, but his face was imperturbable. He plays the part of the loving bridegroom to perfection, she thought bitterly as he pressed her to accept another glass of wine.

'No pearls tonight, my dear?' he enquired.

Georgiana's hand flew to her throat before she remembered. She had laid the pearls back in their case, intending to return them to him.

'They were not suitable with this gown,' she muttered. Her bridal finery, too, was packed away. She could not bear to look at it.

'A pity…but perhaps tomorrow?' There was no warmth in his smile.

Tomorrow you shall have them back, she vowed to herself. She turned away from him and spoke to Richard.

'I hear that you are to go to the West Indies?'

'Yes, Miss Westleigh. I beg your pardon...I should call you sister now that you are Edward's wife.'

'Georgiana will do.' She found that she could not resist his charm. He looked absurdly young as he bent towards her.

'I am to learn to manage the family estates,' he told her with pride. 'I hope I may do well.'

'Of course you will. When do you leave?'

'Quite soon, though Harry goes before me. You will miss him, Georgiana, and so shall I.' His face was wistful. 'I wish we might have gone together, but Edward feels that Harry will do better in the East.'

'I am sure of it.' Edward's voice was bland. 'I have every hope that Harry will become a nabob, if he applies himself.'

Harry beamed upon the assembled company.

'Georgie, I'll make you proud of me.' His eyes sparkled as he looked at her. Then he lowered his voice. 'You don't mind my going, do you?' he asked in an undertone. 'After all, you have Edward now.'

'Yes! I have Edward now.' It took all Georgiana's self-control to utter the words. She shot a swift glance at her husband. It was clear that he had told neither of the young men of their differences. No doubt he was enjoying her discomfiture as she was forced to play out this dreadful charade.

Edward did not look at her. He appeared to be deep in conversation with his brother. She turned again to Harry with a request to be told of his destination in India, and how he would travel there. Later she would be able to remember neither her questions nor his replies.

'Come back, Georgie,' Harry teased. 'You are a world away. I don't believe you've heard a word I've said…'

She made a creditable effort to smile, but her eyes were sad.

'What is it, my dearest? You must not grieve because we are to part for a time. In a year or two you will have your own nursery, and I shall return as the wicked uncle…' He began to laugh.

'I believe you,' she said wryly, though she knew it could never be. His words had served only to remind her of all that she had lost. She blinked back a tear.

'There, there!' Harry patted her hand. 'Edward

will look after you. I was mistaken in him, Georgie. At first I thought you mad, but at bottom he's a stout fellow. He gave us a roasting, though…' His face grew solemn as he recalled the Viscount's biting words.

'He mentioned that he had offered his help,' Georgiana said quietly.

'He will take care of everything. About the money, Georgie… I hope you don't mind. Edward said that as we were brothers now I could accept… He was most insistent.'

'He usually gets his way… But Harry, no more scrapes, do you promise?'

'I give you my word, and I won't break it.'

'Did Edward say what he intended…about Merton?'

'He told us to think no more about the man. I shouldn't care to be in Merton's shoes when Edward meets him. He can be fearsome, can't he? Perhaps he'll manage to get the money back.'

'Perhaps.' Georgiana looked up and caught Richard's eye. He raised his glass to her.

'To the new Viscountess,' he cried gaily. 'When we next see you you'll be at Lyndhurst. I'm beginning to believe the old saw about the ill wind that blows no good.'

'Don't get above yourself, stripling,' Edward's look was enough to cause his brother to subside, but he would not be quelled for long. Relief mingled with excitement as he chattered on about his hopes for both himself and Harry.

Georgiana was bone-weary and depressed, and her head began to ache. For a time she made an effort to join in the conversation, but the pain behind her eyes increased.

'Will you forgive me if I leave you?' she murmured finally.

'Exhausted, my dear?' Edward affected not to notice the smiles of the two young men, but the implication was not lost on Georgiana.

'It has been a long day,' she said stiffly.

'How thoughtless we are!' Harry jumped to his feet. 'Richard, let us go. We may return tomorrow, if Edward will permit...'

'Delighted! You may do me a service, if you will, by acting as Georgiana's escort should she care to see more of the city. I have some matters to attend...'

Georgiana stared at him, and her feeling of depression deepened. Now that Edward had found his brother he had achieved his end in coming to France. She herself was of no further use to him, and she might come and go as she pleased. The knowledge should have brought a feeling of relief, but it left her feeling bereft.

When they were alone she turned to him.

'You have not learned when Merton will return?' she asked coldly.

'Not yet. But let me assure you that you will have no opportunity to warn him…'

'I shall not need to do so. When he seeks out Harry and Richard they will be unable to dissemble.'

'I think not. I have told them what to say.'

'So you have thought of everything? Suppose he should see me in company with my brother in the streets of Paris? He will know at once that something is amiss.'

'You will be in no danger.' Edward's face was imperturbable. 'I have taken steps…'

'So your spies will be at hand? I might have known. I thought it strange that you would set me free.'

He smiled, and she caught her breath.

'I see,' she said slowly. 'You hope that Merton will see us. This is a trap, and I am the bait…'

'Your concern for your friend has quickened your perception, my dear. I congratulate you.'

Green eyes flashing, she took a step towards

him. 'I had not thought that anyone could be so blind,' she cried. 'Merton is not my friend. Would I look kindly on anyone who could harm my brother?'

'You looked rather more than kindly upon me, or have you forgotten your surrender?'

'You need not remind me.' Her colour rose, much to her chagrin. 'There is nothing I regret more bitterly.'

'I do not. It was a most enjoyable experience, and it is more than time that we repeated it.' A vice-like arm slipped about her waist. 'Let me invite you to our bridal bed.'

Georgiana stood like a statue within his grasp.

'I cannot prevent you from taking me, but rape, my lord? You value your honour lightly.'

At that he held her away from him. As the blue eyes looked into hers he was formidable.

'Take care!' he warned. 'You, of all people, may not speak of honour.'

'Of course not! A woman's honour does not weigh with you. What of the lady you betrayed?' She had not forgotten Harry's words, and now she flung them back, too reckless with despair to care for their effect.

Edward's arms fell to his sides. He was white-faced, and his eyes were blazing with anger. Without a word, he strode from the room, leaving Georgiana to enjoy her triumph.

It was a hollow victory. She had wished to drive him away, and she had done so, but it brought her no comfort.

She must get away from him, if only for her own peace of mind. The day when she and Harry sailed for India could not come too soon. I forgot to thank him on Harry's behalf, she thought suddenly. But it did not matter. Doubtless he had some underlying motive for his apparent kindness, even if it was only to separate the two young men.

Her thoughts were bitter as she remembered his courtesy at supper. He could forgive Harry and Richard for their folly, but she herself was not to be excused.

She was well out of her unfortunate marriage, she told herself. Who would wish to be tied for life to such an unpleasant creature? He was arrogant, boorish, unreasonable, and a master of sarcasm. How could she ever have imagined that she loved him? She swallowed the lump in her throat as she rang for Betsy.

Betsy made no comment as her mistress sought

her lonely bed once more, but her face was expressive of surprise.

'His lordship is to make an early start tomorrow.' Georgiana murmured. She did not know if it was true or not, but it would serve as an explanation. At that moment she could not cope with sympathy.

'Then I won't wake you early, madam. You look that fagged…'

'No compliments, Betsy!' Georgiana managed the faintest of smiles. 'A night's sleep will restore me, and my brother is to escort me tomorrow.'

'Mr Harry?' Betsy beamed. It was clear that he had lost none of his ability to charm. 'He'll do you good with his jolly ways.'

Harry's jollity was tested on the following day.

'Notre-Dame? Oh, must we?' He looked dismayed at the prospect. 'You can't wish to poke about a pile of stones, Georgie. We'll have more fun on the river.'

Richard looked relieved at the suggestion, though he had the grace to murmur something about pleasing Georgiana.

'She'll enjoy it,' Harry announced with conviction. 'Won't you, Georgie?'

She did not demur, though the thought crossed

her mind that Edward's spies or bodyguards—whatever he cared to call them—would find it difficult to follow. She did not care.

She looked about her intently as the carriage rolled through the streets, but she saw no signs of pursuit, nor could she distinguish anyone who looked in the least suspicious in the bustling crowds.

As they left the landing-stage several vessels followed in their wake, but they overtook their own slower craft, and Georgiana settled back to enjoy the sensation of the breeze against her face.

'That's better!' Harry glanced at her with approval. 'You looked like a ghost last night. Now you've some colour in your cheeks. Was not this a famous idea?'

'Better than most of yours,' she said drily.

He aimed a playful blow at her. 'No lectures, Georgie. We are both wearing sackcloth today. Richard, ain't that true?'

Richard looked uncomfortable. 'We have both been fools, as Edward pointed out.' He gave her a shy smile. 'But I must thank you for the change in him. He's different somehow. He listened to what we had to say.'

'He'd plenty to say himself.' Harry grimaced. I

may tell you, sister, dear, that he flayed us with his tongue.'

'You may thank your stars that he didn't flay you with a horsewhip.'

'I suppose we deserved it. He was most upset, I believe, by the way I had distressed you, and drawn you in... Oh, Georgie, I am truly sorry.'

She heard his words with some surprise, but, leaning forward, she patted his hand.

'It's over,' she said in an absent tone. 'Now you must think about the future.'

Her words were enough to start both of them into further discussion of their plans, but Georgiana paid them scant attention. As she trailed her fingers in the water she was meditating on Harry's words.

After Edward's rejection of her explanations it seemed strange that he should have berated Harry more for his treatment of his sister than for the fraud which had been the cause of all their troubles. Could she have been mistaken in him?

She pushed the thought aside. Had it not been for her bitter words last night he would have raped her. And he was only too willing to let her go to India with Harry. Those were not the actions of a man in love.

Suddenly she felt chilled.

'It is growing cold,' she said. 'I think we should return.'

They took her back to the hotel, where she presided over a light nuncheon. Then, sensing that they were chafing at the prospect of an afternoon indoors, she announced that she would rest for an hour or two.

'But Edward said…'

'Edward will understand.' She dismissed them and walked into her room.

As she lay down on the bed great waves of sleep came to overwhelm her. She should not have let Harry persuade her to take wine so early in the day, she thought drowsily. Yet it had been only a single glass… She drifted off into slumber.

It was late afternoon when she awoke, and at first she thought she was alone. Then she saw a movement in the chair beside the fireplace.

'Edward?'

'No, my dear. It is not your husband.' Merton rose, stretched, and strolled towards the bed. 'He, I believe, is occupied on some wild-goose chase which I had the foresight to arrange.'

Georgiana lay paralysed. She could not have moved a muscle had she tried.

'What a clever little creature you are!' The silvery eyes were mere slits as they gazed down at her. 'It is a pity that your brother has not more of your intelligence.'

'I don't know what you mean,' she breathed.

'Oh, come now! To marry the Viscount, throwing him off the scent—it was a master-stroke!'

'You may not always think it so. He is no fool.'

'Agreed! That is what makes him such a worthy adversary. Now, my dear, let us to business.'

'I have no business with you.'

'On the contrary, I think you have. My dear Viscountess, do you believe that I will allow your husband to destroy my plans?'

'He knows everything. You cannot keep your villainy a secret.'

'Dead men tell no tales,' he said sententiously. 'An old saw, but a true one...'

Georgiana laughed in his face.

'My lord will not be taken easily...'

'Your faith in him is touching. Such devotion! I believe you would do anything to keep him safe.'

She did not reply, but her eyes never left his face.

'You will not save him, I assure you. Even now it needs but a word from me and he is a dead man.'

'Why do you hate him so?' she cried in anguish.

'Is it not enough that you have ruined his brother and my own?'

'It gave me some satisfaction, but the game is not yet played to its conclusion. Lyndhurst will pay in full for the injury he has done.'

'I don't know what you mean. He has not injured you…'

'No?' The cruel mouth twisted in a grimace. 'You know little of the man you married, my dear. He is a master of deception, as my sister found to her cost.'

Georgiana gazed at him in horror.

'He was to marry her,' Merton continued. 'The announcement appeared in the *Morning Chronicle* and on that promise she allowed herself to be seduced. Your gallant knight then abandoned her and she killed herself.'

'Oh, no!' Georgiana's hand flew to her mouth as if to stifle a cry of anguish. 'You must be mistaken about him. He could not do such a thing.'

'You have not known him long, I believe. In time you will learn the truth.'

'I trust him,' she said with spirit. 'Again I say that you will not find it easy to destroy him.'

'Perhaps not, but then…I have a hostage.'

Georgiana laughed again.

'You are mistaken, sir, if you think this marriage other than a sham. The Viscount does not care for me. His intention was to find his brother.'

'Madam, you are either very clever or a fool.' The silvery eyes were fixed upon her face. 'Shall we put it to the test? Let us approach the Viscount with a proposition; your life or your death...'

'That won't be necessary.' Lyndhurst stepped from behind the concealing curtain. He held a pistol in each hand. 'Stand back, sir. You will please to sit down over there.' He gestured towards a writing table.

Merton shrugged. He had betrayed no surprise at Edward's sudden appearance, but the twitching of an eyelid belied his iron self-control.

'Be careful, Edward! I'm sure he is armed,' Georgiana warned.

'Undoubtedly, my dear. You will take out your pistol very slowly, sir, and lay it on the table.'

Merton did as he was bidden, but he did not speak. Apparently at his ease, he lolled back in his chair, gazing at Edward with a smile of contempt.

Georgiana watched as her husband walked towards him. Edward had never looked more formidable, but she was terrified. As Merton tensed she gave a cry of fright. Keeping a safe distance between himself and the man across the table, Edward picked up the pistol. Then he jerked his head towards the door to the parlour.

'We shall discuss our business elsewhere,' he said coolly. 'I have no wish to distress my wife.' He motioned to Merton to precede him.

The door had scarcely closed behind them before Georgiana was out of bed. She dressed in great haste, almost crying with exasperation as she tugged at recalcitrant ribbons and knots.

Edward had indicated that she must not join them, but she could not wait to find out what might happen. She hurried to the door, half fearing to hear a shot, but only a murmur of conversation was audible. Both men were speaking in low tones, and she could not distinguish a word.

She reached for the handle of the door, hoping to open it the merest crack. Then she stopped. If it creaked and Edward's attention was distracted his enemy would seize the chance to overpower him. Merton, she knew, would snuff out her husband's life without a second thought.

In an agony of mind she waited for what seemed like hours. She knew that she should get help, but Harry and Richard had sought their lodgings hours ago. She did not know where to find them, and in any case she could not roam the streets in the hours of darkness.

Scroggins, perhaps? He was devoted to his master, though she did not know if he could handle a gun. But it might be better than nothing. She reached out for the bell-rope, then hesitated. Edward might not wish to involve the man, and he might not welcome her interference.

The waiting was torture, but there was nothing she could do. She was sick with anxiety; her mind was racing. How much had Edward heard of her conversation with Merton? She tried to recall each word that had passed between them. They had not troubled to lower their voices, and Edward had been there from the start. He must have entered her room whilst she slept.

The tight feeling in her chest began to ease. Now, at least, Edward would know that Merton was as much her enemy as his. He must have suspected that the man would come for her, if not that night then another. But how had he guessed that she would be alone?

The blood in her veins seemed to turn to ice. Perhaps he had not known. He might have hoped to find them both asleep.

She stifled a cry. To take her he must have come

prepared to kill her husband. Even now they might be struggling… She ran to the door again, but the voices had stopped and there was silence.

A vision of Edward's lifeless body lying in the other room spurred her to action, and she flung the door wide. In the candlelight she saw Edward standing by the table reading a document. He was alone. Her relief was so great that she thought her legs would not support her as she stumbled towards him.

'My love!' In two quick strides he was across the room to gather her into his arms.

'I thought he must have killed you,' she sobbed.

'I had the pistols, little goose! Had you forgotten?'

'He might have had another…in his sleeve or in his boot…' She would not be comforted.

'I had not overlooked the possibility, my dearest. I'm only surprised that you did not join us to remind me…' His tone was severe, but when she looked into his eyes she found that he was laughing.

She bridled. 'I don't always interfere, whatever you may think,' she told him stiffly.

'But you were tempted…? Come now, admit it!'

'I was afraid for you,' she said simply. 'Merton is a dangerous man.'

'His fangs are drawn.' Edward sat down and

took her upon his knee. 'He may not return to England. I have his confession, and also a letter to his bankers.' He pointed to the documents.

'But how…?'

'Don't ask, my love. It is better that you do not know the lengths to which your husband is prepared to go to keep you safe.'

'I thought you might have been forced to shoot him.'

'There are other methods of persuasion…and I am not without influence in certain quarters. Like all bullies, he collapsed when faced with the inevitable.'

Georgiana shook her head. 'I can't be easy in my mind,' she murmured. 'He agreed too quickly.'

He silenced her with a long kiss. Then he lifted her in his arms and carried her to her room.

Chapter Eleven

'Georgiana, I have much to say to you. Are you too tired to listen to me tonight?' Edward sat beside her, holding her hand.

She shook her head. 'I should not sleep.'

'Merton has told you an ugly tale. I should have spoke of it myself, but it happened years ago and I had no wish to distress you…'

She put a finger to his lips to silence him. 'Do not go on,' she said. 'There is no need…'

'But I want you to know the truth of it. I did know Merton's sister, though I did not guess at their relationship until tonight. She was a widow, with a husband dead in the Peninsular War.' He hesitated, frowning. 'The lady wished to remarry, and I seemed a suitable candidate, though we were mere acquaintances.'

'My dearest, this is painful for you. I wish you would not…'

'Dear Georgie, hear me out… When I did not come up to scratch she took matters into her own hands. It was she who sent the announcement to the papers and when I desired her to retract she accused me of seduction. It was an ugly business, but I was forced to insist. The next I knew was that she had killed herself.'

'How terrible! She must have been unbalanced.'

'There is some history of insanity in the family, I believe.'

'Yes, Harry told me that Merton himself is sometimes…other than normal.'

'I don't doubt it. Georgie, this is why I had to force his hand.'

'You knew he would come for me tonight?'

'I could not be sure, but I felt that if he heard that we had quarrelled he might seize the opportunity. Betsy was given leave to spread the news.'

'How long had you been behind the curtain?' she asked shyly.

'Long enough to hear how much you love me.'

His look was a tribute to her courage. 'I came in whilst you slept.'

'My darling, I have been guilty of dissembling. I've caused you pain, and for that I shall not easily forgive myself. I could think of no other way to trap Merton than to let him think that I did not share your bed.'

'Your anger was convincing,' she admitted ruefully.

He stroked her cheek. 'It was not entirely simulated. When Harry and Richard told me that you had agreed to Merton's plans I could not believe it.'

'I was trying to save your life.'

'I know that now.' Exasperation mingled with amusement in his expression as he looked at her. 'But could you not trust me enough to tell me what you knew?'

'I wanted to, but I didn't know what to do. Both you and Harry were at risk, and Richard too.'

'So you were prepared to carry the burden alone?' Edward took her hand in his. 'That must not happen in future.'

'Then you have forgiven me?' Her head was bent and she could not look at him.

He tilted her face to his and dropped a kiss upon her nose. 'That question needs no answer. Did it not seem strange to you that I could be on terms with Harry and my brother, and yet so distant with my wife?'

'You were more than distant,' she reproached. 'I hated you for your cruelty.'

'My darling, I ran grave risks, but our marriage was common knowledge. Merton, I knew, would be aware of it as soon as he returned. When he could not find Richard and Harry he would be forced to come to you.'

'But he knew where they lived…'

'I persuaded them to change their lodgings.' He gave her a quizzical look. 'I hoped that he, knowing that we were at odds with each other, would believe that you would be easily convinced…'

'Never!'

'He did not know that, and Betsy followed my instructions. She let it be known that tonight I would not share your bed.'

'To find you here would not have stopped him.' Georgiana's eyes were haunted. 'You might have been asleep…'

'Asleep? With you to tempt me?' His glowing look brought hot colour flooding to her face. Then, with a sigh, he rose. 'You will think about my words? I have treated you so badly, Georgiana. I shall not blame you if you still wish to go with Harry. Remember only that I love you more than life.'

'Dearest Edward, that is all I need to know.' Blindly she reached out for him. 'Don't leave me now. I cannot bear to be without you for a single hour.'

He caught her to him, murmuring endearments as he showered kisses upon her face. That night their passion knew no bounds, and the bond between them grew with each tender word of love. It was full daylight before they slept.

Georgiana awakened first. Carefully she raised herself on one elbow to gaze at Edward's face. In sleep he looked endearingly vulnerable. She was tempted to reach out and brush back the tousled curls which had fallen on to his brow, but she would not disturb him.

She smiled to herself. She had no need to study that beloved face to recall the laughter-lines at the corners of his eyes, the clean line of his jaw, or the curve of that mobile mouth. How long his lashes were...

He stirred, and as he turned towards her the sheet which covered him fell aside. Georgiana looked in wonder at his magnificent physique. She had lost all her shyness at the sight of his naked body. This man was hers alone, and she knew every inch of those perfect contours, from the broad shoulders which tapered to a trim waist, to the long, heavily muscled legs.

Gently she rested her cheek against his chest. Then she gasped as his arms closed round her.

'I thought you were asleep,' she protested. 'You were deceiving me again.' Her eyes were filled with laughter.

'Not so, my temptress!' He held her comfortingly close, and kissed her soundly. 'I have been watching you!' he teased. 'Are you happy with your bargain?'

She blushed. 'I…I did not mean to stare at you, but you are so dear to me. I could not ask for more…'

'Not even more of the same?' He reached out for her and she could not mistake the look in his eyes. She evaded his grasp, slipped out of bed, and fled across the room, still laughing.

'I did not mean…what you thought I meant.' she cried in confusion.

'Come here. You know that you promised to obey me.'

'It is very late. What Betsy will think I can't imagine.'

'I can. And, madam, that demure look is quite

out of place when you are mother-naked.' He was out of bed and striding towards her.

'Edward, please… We ought to make an appearance… Suppose Harry and Richard should arrive?'

'They may go away again.' He made a grab for her, but she ran to stand behind a chair.

'You won't escape me,' he promised as he pushed it aside.

'I will…I will.' She shrieked as he caught her, and collapsed in gales of laughter.

'Such a disobedient wife! What am I to do with you?' He lifted her in his arms.

'Perhaps more of the same?' she murmured, greatly daring, but unashamed of her longing for him.

Betsy, coming to wake her mistress, heard the laughter and went away again.

For Georgiana the rest of the day had a dream-like quality. She dressed and breakfasted and welcomed Harry and Richard when they came to dine, but her thoughts were all of Edward. Her happiness was overwhelming.

Lost in love, she was only half-aware of the conversation of her companions. Then Harry turned to her with sparkling eyes.

'Is it not splendid that Edward routed Merton? He even got the money, Georgie, though I don't know how he did it.' He shot a speculative look at his brother-in-law.

'He will not tell you. I asked, but it seems that we are not to know.' Georgiana smiled at Edward.

'Let me keep my secrets,' Edward teased. 'It is enough that he will trouble us no further.'

'Yet I find it strange... I had not thought he would give in without a struggle.'

Georgiana frowned at her brother's persistence, though she could understand his misgivings. She felt a tiny stirring of apprehension. Had she not felt the same?

She shook her head as if to clear it of unpleasant thoughts. She would trust in Edward's judgement but try as she might she could not forget their enemy. Merton had terrified her beyond all reason, and the memory of those hooded eyes still had the power to turn her blood to ice.

Always, in his presence, she had felt that she was screaming inwardly. From their first meeting she had sensed that there was something strange about him...something which another human being could not reach. A sick mind had to be a cause for pity, but with Merton it was more than that. For the first time in her life she had come face to face with evil. She began to shiver.

'Are you cold, my dearest?' Edward moved to close the open window.

Georgiana shook her head. She must keep a closer guard upon her thoughts. Edward must not guess that the mere mention of Merton's name was enough to terrify her.

His keen eyes searched her face. Then he turned the conversation into lighter channels. It was not until late that night as he lay beside her that he spoke again of Merton.

'My love, are you still afraid?' he began.

Startled, she looked up at him. 'I...I... No, of course not.'

'I wonder how I ever imagined that you could cheat and lie,' he said lightly as he twisted a straying curl about his fingers. 'Your face is the mirror of your thoughts, my darling. When Merton's name is mentioned that haunted look returns. I had hoped to banish it forever.'

'I wish I could believe that he will not return,' she told him wistfully. 'Will you not tell me what you said to him?'

Edward looked at her thoughtfully. 'I had hoped to keep it from you. You will not think well of me, though I had the right…and I would do more, much more, to keep you safe.'

'So…please tell me.'

'I have some papers in my possession,' he said slowly. 'They are from his sister…letters and…and the final suicide note. They prove beyond doubt that she was mad. I kept them long ago to still the gossips' tongues, but I did not. She was gone, and I would not sully the reputation of the dead.'

Georgiana cradled his head upon her breast. 'I love you for that,' she said softly.

'There is more.' Edward's voice was low. 'There was a son…Merton's nephew and the son of her dead husband. The boy is kept hidden at the family home. He is a lunatic. Even as a child there were ugly stories concerning his treatment of various animals. I will not distress you with the details. Now the lad is seventeen and he is dangerous and cunning. He has a keeper, but sometimes he escapes…'

'Oh, Edward…'

'Do you wish me to go on?'

Georgiana nodded though his face was so grim that she dreaded to hear what he would tell her.

'There have been attacks…first upon children and then upon the village girls…'

'How do you know of this?'

'His dead father's estate runs alongside my own. That was how I came to meet the lady. His grandparents live there now, but they are no longer young, and they cannot control the boy.

'I went to see them before I left for the West Indies, and obtained a promise that he would be moved to a place of safety where he could do no further harm, but that did not happen.'

'Why not? It would seem the sensible thing to do.'

'My bailiff tells me that someone stepped in and persuaded them against it.'

'Merton?'

'It must have been Merton. He is the boy's only other living relative. I had never met him, but I'd been aware for some time that someone with influence was covering up the attacks. Now there has been a murder.'

Georgiana sat up suddenly. 'You must speak out at once,' she said with conviction. 'Inform the authorities; they will know what to do.'

'I had every intention of laying the case before them,' Edward told her with a look of pain. 'Then I found out who Merton was. My dear, it was the only weapon I could use against him.'

'The threat of exposure?'

'Yes. I said that I would inform against him.'

'But Edward, you must. Not even to save Richard, Harry or myself shall you leave a lunatic at large, to murder as he wills.'

'He will not be left at large. One of my conditions is that Merton does as I suggest and arranges for the boy to be kept secure. The alternatives are Bedlam, or, at worst, the hangman's rope.'

Georgiana paled. 'Oh, they would not hang him?'

'It is a possibility, and I cannot decide if it would be the better fate…'

She was silent then. How often she had spoken out in indignation against those members of the London *ton* who sought amusement in that infamous place, laughing and scoffing at the spectacle of the Bedlamites and their curious antics. The thought of the gallows outside Newgate made her tremble.

'I understand now,' she whispered. 'You forced him to agree to your terms, but, Edward, you will always be a danger to him, and he has his bully boys. I shall not soon forget the men who attacked you.'

'Yet I too have my "bully boys", as you so rightly term them. Since I knew the truth you have not been out of their sight.'

'I did not notice them.'

'You were not supposed to. I durst not risk another scold for setting spies on you.' His eyes twinkled.

'Do you think me a termagant?' she demanded.

'I think you adorable. Now let me kiss away that troubled look.'

He was as good as his word, and it was some time before they slept.

It was the smell of smoke which roused her. She laid a hand on Edward's shoulder.

'What is it, my love?'

'Smoke! Do you not smell smoke?'

He was out of bed in an instant. 'Get dressed,' he said quickly. He wasted no time in pulling on his shirt, breeches and coat. 'I will find out what is happening.'

As he opened the door she heard shouting and the sound of running feet. Beyond him she could see a mob of struggling figures in the corridor.

Georgiana grabbed her pearls and her reticule. Then she began to stuff clothing into a bag.

'Leave that,' Edward ordered sharply. He stepped into the corridor with outstretched arms, bringing the crowd to a halt.

'You will run less risk of injury if you walk quietly to the staircase,' he said in a calm voice. His words had a steadying effect, and he turned to a man who seemed cooler than the others. 'What has happened?'

'Fire, sir. It started at the far end of the building and is moving fast. You had best go now if you wish to save your skin.'

'The place is alight, my dear.' Edward turned back to Georgiana. 'We must go at once.'

'What of Betsy…and Scroggins? Are they not at the top of the building?'

'I have not forgotten them, Georgie. Let me take you to safety, then I shall go back for them.'

She hesitated.

'Is there not time for you to find them? The smoke is thick, but there are no flames…'

'I won't risk your safety, Georgie. Come with me. For all we know they may already have escaped.' He took her hand and led her into the corridor.

The first wild rush of fleeing guests had ended, and they were passed only by single half-clad figures who hurried by with cloths pressed against their mouths.

Georgiana began to cough and choke. Her eyes were streaming from the effects of smoke. Without pausing in his stride Edward stripped off his coat and threw it about her head.

The fire was gaining on them. She tried to run as she heard crackling and the smell of burning wood. Behind them the tinder-dry wainscoting went up in a shower of sparks.

'Take your time.' Edward caught at her arm to slow her down. 'We are almost there.'

Even as he spoke she heard a crash, accompanied by agonised screaming.

'No, don't look!' Edward buried her face in his shoulder as he glanced into the yawning pit at his feet. 'The staircase has collapsed. We must find another way.'

He could prevent her from seeing the full horror of the tragedy, but the shrieks of the scorched and mutilated victims followed them as they turned back along the corridor. A strange smell hung on the air. It was that of burning flesh, and Georgiana felt her gorge rise.

'This way!' Edward had found another corridor leading to the right. The smoke was thickening fast, but as yet there were no flames. With an arm about her shoulders he urged her along. Then she heard a wave of sound behind her. She looked round and gave a cry of fright as a terror-stricken mob bore down upon them.

In a second she lost her grip on Edward's hand

as the crowd engulfed them. She turned her head and saw him vainly trying to plead for calm, but hysteria had overcome the fleeing guests. His words of entreaty fell upon deaf ears. Then he was by her side again.

'It is useless,' he said quietly. Protecting her with his body, he forced a way to the edge of the crowd. 'In here, my love...' He thrust her into one of the rooms leading off the corridor and closed the door behind him.

'We shall be trapped,' she cried wildly.

'Not so!' He strode across to the window and flung it wide. Then he nodded in satisfaction. 'Thank heavens there is a balcony.'

She hurried across to join him, clutching him to her as she took great gulps of air. Gently he disengaged her fingers.

'I want you to be brave, my love. There is another balcony below. It is not too far for me to lower you closer to the ground.'

'No! I can't do it.' Georgiana looked down to the street below, and the distance to the ground appalled her. 'I'm afraid. I've always been afraid of heights. I shall fall, I know it.'

'You will not fall, I promise.' He pulled a sheet from the bed and tore it into strips. 'See, I will fasten this around your waist and tie it to a chest. Then you will be quite safe.'

'Can't we stay here and wait for help? Look, someone has already fetched a ladder!'

It was true. There was much activity in the watching crowd which filled the street.

'The ladders will not reach to the second floor. Besides, they are made of wood…'

She did not need to be told what would happen if the wood should catch fire.

'But they are bringing water too,' she pleaded. 'I can see men with buckets…'

'They will not douse this conflagration. Georgie, look at me!'

Obediently she raised her eyes to his.

'My love, in this at least you must obey me. Will you do as I say?'

Dumb with terror, she could only nod.

'That's my darling girl!' Deftly he knotted the sheet about her waist, and tied the other end securely to a heavy piece of furniture.

'Edward!' Her soul was in her eyes, and he caught her to him with a muffled groan. 'My love, you will follow me?'

'I will…I promise.' He leaned over the balcony.

'I can see no smoke from below. It seems likely that the fire was started on this floor.'

'But if it is spreading...?'

'When you reach the balcony go at once to the door of the room. If it is open you must close it. The wood will take some time to burn. Soak sheets and covers if you can find some water and pile them against the jamb. That will buy some time.'

'But...but I thought you said that you would follow me.'

'I will...but you must make a start.' To still any further protests he gave her a long kiss. Then he took her in his arms and lifted her over the balcony sill.

'Don't look down,' he ordered. 'Keep your eyes on me.' His hands were like bands of iron as he gripped her wrists. 'Down you go,' he said cheerfully.

Georgiana made her mind a blank as he swung her into space. She could not scream. Her throat was too constricted, but the steady hands still held her, and she was conscious of their immense strength.

'Can you feel the edge of the balcony?' Edward asked in a conversational tone.

'Y-yes,' she whispered.

'Then swing your feet inside it and I'll release you. Tell me when you have done so.'

'Now.' She offered a silent prayer as her wrists were freed. Then she was on solid ground again.

'Are you safe, my love?' Edward's deep voice was reassuring.

'Yes, but please hurry.'

'I shall be with you in a moment. Do you untie the sheet from about your waist.'

It was a struggle to loosen the knots. They had tightened even further as they had taken the strain of her weight, but she managed at last.

'It's free,' she called.

The end of the sheet flapped idly in the breeze, but there was silence from above.

'Edward?' Her voice was high with panic. She leaned out as far as she could, striving to catch a glimpse of him, but the floor of the upper balcony blocked her view.

Where could he be? She could not think what had happened. Had he been overcome by smoke? In an agony of mind she called to him again and again, but he did not reply.

In desperation she looked at the flapping rope of sheets, but she was forced to dismiss the idea of climbing up again. It was beyond her strength.

There might be another way to reach him. She ran to the door and opened it. There was a strong smell of smoke in the corridor, but the air was clear. She stepped outside just as the first grey wisps curled towards her from the angle of the staircase. To her fevered imagination the smoke was like some malevolent spirit, reaching out to claim her life. She closed the door on it.

What could she do? Edward's words came back to her. Had he not said that she must pile up soaking bedding?

Working quickly, she snatched up the coverlet and threw it against the door. Thankfully the enormous waterjug on the dressing stand was full, but she could not lift it. She seized a vase from the mantelshelf, dipping it into the jug again and again until the contents had reduced the bedding to a sodden mass.

Sheets? She took those too, but the waterjug was almost empty. Fiercely she trampled them into the coverlet until they too were soaking. In her haste she tripped and fell against the door, realising with a gasp that the ancient oak panels were hot enough to burn her skin. The fire had travelled more quickly than she could possibly have imagined.

Frantic now, she ran back to the balcony but her shouts to Edward went unanswered. Again she craned her neck out far beyond the balustrade, but a shower of burning debris from above drove her back indoors. Then the upper balcony gave way and fell in a flaming mass to the street below.

Georgiana fought a rising tide of hysteria. She must be calm. If she panicked now it might cost her her life. The smoke in the room was no thicker, and the door, though hot to the touch, was not yet alight.

Edward must have decided to find another way to reach her. She would not believe that he had succumbed to the flames. It wasn't possible. He was wise and resourceful. Perhaps even now he was trying to reach her from the street.

If she could only see him… She eyed her balcony doubtfully. The deadly shower of burning fragments had stopped, and it seemed safe enough to venture out…

She gave a cry. The floor was smouldering. She kicked wildly at the charred debris which was setting it alight, sighing with relief as she realised that she had caught it in time.

Others were not so fortunate. The noise was deafening as screams of terror mingled with an ominous crackling as the fire took hold. Piteous cries for help issued from almost every window, though many were stilled by a crash behind them as the floors gave way.

The upper floor was well alight and smoke and flames belched forth from balconies. Was no one trying to help them?

She looked down into the street. Some ladders had been placed against the building, but they were woefully short. She saw men lashing two or three together in an effort to reach the upper floors, but a sudden burst of flame from one of the windows caught the first climber and sent him screaming to the ground. In seconds the ladder was alight.

Buckets of water werc being passed from hand to hand along a chain of sweating men, but she knew that they could not reach her.

She stepped back quickly as something hurtled past her. Then she closed her eyes. Someone had jumped.

The blazing figure was followed by others…all of them missing the outstretched blankets held by willing hands.

Georgiana could not stop shaking. Nausea threatened to overcome her at the thought of those hideous deaths. She would not jump, but perhaps she could lower herself to safety in the way that Edward had lowered her from the floor above.

It was her only chance. She must ignore her

fear of heights. It seemed unimportant when weighed against the prospect of death by fire.

And it was not so very far to the ground from this floor. If she could attract attention the men below might catch her if she fell.

The sodden sheets were difficult to make into a rope but she forced her trembling fingers to obey her. She blessed the day that Harry had shown her how to tie a knot securely.

She used up all the cloth she had and secured one end to the bed. The other she wound about her waist. Silently she prayed that it was long enough and would hold. Then she walked on to the balcony and waved her arms above her head.

Edward would see her, she was sure... But there was no sign of his tall figure in the crowd. Then she caught sight of Betsy's tear-stained face. Half-clad, the girl was standing beside her uncle, sobbing bitterly as she looked up at the building.

As she saw Georgiana her expression changed. She grabbed at Scroggins' arm, pointing upwards in excitement.

Scroggins did not hesitate. He started to run towards the hotel entrance, but a dozen men held him back. Shouting and gesticulating, he could not break their hold, and Georgiana was glad of it. He must not risk his life for her.

At least she had been seen. In seconds a blanket was in place beneath her balcony. The time had come to take her courage in both hands. A hush fell on the crowd below.

She took a deep breath and was about to trust herself to the makeshift rope when she heard shouting from the corridor. The sound was distant, but it could only mean that someone had found a way through. Edward was coming for her, she was sure of it.

With shaking fingers she tore at the rope about her waist, trying to loosen it. The cloth was stiff and intractable, but the knots came apart at last.

She ran to the door, calling as she went. Feverishly she tore at the sodden coverlet which blocked the door, kicking aside pillows and cushions in her haste. Even as she worked the door began to open, slowly at first, as it met the barrier of her makeshift seal, and then more quickly.

Clouds of smoke billowed into the room, causing her to gasp for breath. She ignored the choking sensation in her throat, but her eyes were streaming as she reached out to the dimly seen figure of her rescuer.

'Edward!' she cried on a sob. 'Oh, my love, I thought I had lost you…'

But it was not Edward who came towards her through the smoke. She looked into Merton's face and then she screamed.

Chapter Twelve

Merton's eyes were blank and Georgiana knew then that he was quite mad. He gripped her arm above the elbow and led her back to the balcony.

'Is this not a wonderful sight? A foretaste of hell! I had not thought to see the like when I first lit the kindling.'

'You? It was you who started this?'

'Oh yes! Just a small diversion…but now it is magnificent. I feel like a god!' He threw his arms to heaven in a gesture of triumph.

Georgiana turned to run, but he was too quick for her. Again he caught her arm.

'Don't go! It is not over yet. See, the wall is about to collapse…' He laughed aloud as part of the building bulged and then fell, driving the spectators back.

'But the people…the guests…? Had you no thought for them?'

'They are enjoying it,' he assured her solemnly. 'See how they jump out of the windows. It must be like flying… Would you like to try?'

Georgiana did not shrink from him. She must not show her fear. If she could but keep him talking…

'Not yet,' she said. 'It is not quite over, as you told me.'

'But you were screaming,' he demurred. 'I thought it did not please you…'

'I did not like the flames at first,' she said quickly. 'I thought they must burn me.'

'But they are beautiful!' He sounded puzzled. 'They are the colour of your hair.' He reached up and laid his hand upon her curls.

Georgiana stood very still. Her instinct was to run, but it would be useless. She would not get far.

Merton turned back to the spectacle before him. For a time he watched intently, a cry of pleasure escaping his lips as one wall after another burned and fell. Then he frowned and his face darkened.

'They are spoiling it.' He pointed to a corner of the building where the fire sputtered out as men threw water on the blaze.

'I'll stop them.' He gnawed at his lower lip. 'Yes, I'll stop them just as I stopped the other one.'

Georgiana had a dreadful premonition.

'The...the other one?' she breathed. 'Who was that?'

'He wanted the torch,' Merton muttered vaguely. 'He tried to take it, but I was too clever for him. When he turned to put it out I struck him down.'

Georgiana forgot her fear of him. She tugged at his coat.

'Who was it?' she cried. 'Did you know him?'

At last she had his full attention. He bent his gaze upon her and something moved at the back of the silvery eyes...something as insubstantial as a cloud reflected in a still pool.

Then the thin lips curled back in a travesty of a smile. 'He was my enemy,' he told her. 'And yours as well. I saw him trying to throw you from the balcony. I was standing behind the statue over there...' He pointed across the square.

Georgiana's head was reeling. The floor was behaving oddly. It seemed to be coming up to meet her. Oh, God, she must not faint...

'Why did you come back?' she cried in anguish.

'I wanted to be sure that he would burn in hell.

I killed him, but he did not suffer. I am not cruel, only just…I carried out the sentence…'

Georgiana could not speak. A lump formed in her throat as she gazed at him with horror in her eyes.

Merton gave her a guileless smile. 'I can make a torch for you,' he offered. 'Then we can go together to the other rooms. You will like that. The wood catches fire at once, and then it crackles and speaks to me.'

Despair filled her heart. With Edward gone she had no wish to live, but the instinct for survival was strong. Even in her sorrow she dreaded the thought of death by fire.

In desperation she looked about her for some weapon; the candlesticks on the mantelshelf looked heavy enough…but if she did not succeed with her first blow Merton would kill her there and then. He had all the strength of a madman.

The breeze was freshening now, and it had changed direction. There were cries from below as sparks flew across to the neighbouring buildings.

Merton watched with avid interest. Then he turned and made for the door, dragging her behind him.

'Quickly!' he said. 'We must help them, or our enemies will put it out.'

The corridor was filled with choking smoke. It was so thick that she could not see a yard ahead of her.

'No!' She struggled to break his grip. 'Let us go back. We shall be overcome...'

'Don't be afraid.' Merton's voice was almost kindly. 'I know the way to the other building. See, I have the key.' He opened his clenched fist to show it to her.

'Where did you find that?'

He gave her a cunning smile. 'I stole it before...before... I have forgotten...let me think.' He frowned and then his face cleared. 'I remember now,' he said. 'You promised to come away with me. I stole it so that we could get away.'

Georgiana thought fast. Merton must have had the key for some time.

'I'm glad,' she said simply. 'How clever you are! Is that how you got into the building...from the house next door?'

He did not answer her. He was moving so fast that she had to run to keep up with him. Then she stumbled and fell, breaking his grip as she did so.

He cursed as he raised her to her feet, but the fall had given her an idea. If she could break his grip again she would disappear into the smoke.

She took a few more steps and fell again, squirming out of his grasp. Then she sprang to her feet and began to run in the opposite direction. If she could but find the room again, or even another one, she might yet escape him.

She had no idea where she was. Her eyes were stinging and she could see nothing. Blindly she reached out and touched the wainscoting on one wall. It was hot, but she ignored the pain as she trailed her fingers along, searching for a doorjamb or a latch.

There, she had it… But before she could open the door a hand closed about her mouth and she was held in a fierce grip.

'Georgie!' Edward's arms went round her. 'Thank God I've found you.'

Georgiana peered up at him in disbelief as joy swept through her. Edward was alive, though clearly he was badly injured. The face which she loved so well was now a bloody mask, blackened with smoke.

'Where is Merton?' he asked quickly.

'He is out there somewhere.' She pointed along the corridor. 'Edward, he has a key to the building next door. That is how he comes and goes. It is an escape route.'

'Then let us follow him.' He put his arm about her shoulders, but she saw at once that he could move only with difficulty.

'Would it not be best to go back to the room again?'

'It is an inferno. I jumped down to the balcony, but the flames had taken hold. I thought is must give beneath my weight...'

She did not question him further. Whatever happened now they were together. The danger was great, but she was conscious only of an overwhelming sense of relief. At least he was alive.

Their progress along the corridor was painfully slow. Georgiana had her arm about Edward's waist, but she found it difficult to support his weight as he leaned ever more heavily upon her. She looked at him with anxious eyes.

'Can you go on?' she murmured.

'To the end, if need be,' he assured her. 'See, Georgie, the air is clearing.'

It was true. Perceptibly the smoke was thinning as they moved along.

Georgiana scarcely dared to hope. Could it be that they were close to rescue? Her eyes were shining as she looked at Edward's face.

'Just a few more steps, my darling,' she encouraged. 'Then we shall be safe…' Her words died on her lips as Merton blocked their path. He looked at Edward in wonder.

'I killed you,' he said. 'Why won't you die?'

A pistol appeared in his hand as if by magic as Edward lunged towards him.

'Don't make me shoot you,' Merton pleaded. 'That would be wrong. You are to die in the fire.'

Georgiana's mind was racing. 'How can that be?' she said gently. 'Look about you. There are no flames in this part of the building.'

'That's true!' Merton shook his head as if to clear it. 'The flames are in your hair, but they won't kill him…' He frowned at her. 'I lost you back there…and we were going…we were going…'

'We were going to see the other fire,' Georgiana prompted. 'You promised me that…don't you recall?'

He considered for a moment. 'I think so…'

'Then should we not make haste? Otherwise your enemies will put it out.'

'But he is my enemy.' He waved the pistol at Edward. 'I want to see him burn.'

'Have you forgotten the way to lead us to the other fire?' Georgiana made a desperate attempt to divert his attention from Edward. 'You told me that you had a key.'

'I have…' He swung the heavy object from one finger, holding it tantalisingly out of reach. 'But I must keep it.'

'Of course you must, if you are to use it. Shall we go?'

'I…I don't know…' He sounded puzzled. 'There was something I had to do.' His glance fell on Edward, and again Georgiana saw the strange stirring in his eyes.

'The fire!' she cried in desperation. 'Don't forget the fire…'

'That's it!' He smiled at her. 'I can burn him there… Come…we are wasting time…'

He motioned them ahead of him, his pistol pressed firmly into Edward's spine.

Georgiana still had her arm about her husband's waist, supporting his stumbling steps. He bent towards her.

'Georgie, when you see the chance you must run,' he whispered.

She shook her head. 'I won't leave you.'

'You must. I'm not as weak as I appear.'

She did not look at him. If what he said was true she must not arouse Merton's suspicions. She began to stoop as if Edward's weight were too much for her. Coughing and choking, she staggered along the corridor. In that at least she had no need to dissemble. Her stinging eyes were streaming from the effect of the smoke. Then it began to clear.

Georgiana felt a flicker of hope. To reach the adjoining building Merton would be forced to lead them across the square outside. He could not disguise the fact that Edward was injured, and that she herself was on the verge of collapse. Had he not realised that help would be at hand?

Her hopes were soon dashed. As she turned to the staircase leading to the hotel entrance Merton stopped her.

'Not that way!' His eyes were cunning. 'My enemies are out there…'

He pushed them ahead of him along a corridor leading to the rear, taking a key from his pocket as he did so. The heat was intense and Georgiana winced with each step she took. Her think kid slippers offered no protection from the scorching floorboards.

Edward's arm tightened about her shoulders. 'Be ready!' he warned.

Georgiana needed no persuading. She might have been standing in the open doorway of a furnace. At any moment she feared that the floor and the walls would ignite. She was soaked to the skin in sweat.

Then they were forced to stop at the end of the corridor. A massive door barred their way. Merton walked around them carefully, keeping them at a distance.

With a groan Edward sank to the ground. His collapse was so realistic that Georgiana gave a cry of anguish and fell to her knees beside him.

Merton eyed them without interest. He kicked at the inert figure, but there was no response. Satisfied, he turned to open the door.

'Down!' Edward shouted. He threw his arms about Georgiana and rolled her to one side, covering her with his body as a wall of fire belched out towards them.

Merton stood no chance. His hair and clothing burst into flame as he was caught by the inferno. With arms outstretched he screamed in mortal agony as he fell into the blaze.

Then Edward was on his feet, slamming the door on the horrific sight. Without a word he seized Georgiana's arm and hurried her away.

She felt sick and faint but he did not slow his pace. 'We are almost there,' he encouraged. 'Don't fail me now. The fire can move more quickly than a man can run.'

Terror lent wings to her feet, but even so it seemed an age before they stumbled out into the sunlight. As the sound of cheering reached her ears Georgiana fainted.

She returned to consciousness to find herself resting in the cool luxury of lavender-scented sheets. There was a strange taste in her mouth which she could not recognise. Then full memory returned. She could still taste and smell acrid smoke.

In a panic she sat bolt upright. Where was Edward? Were they safe, or was this building too in the path of the fire? She cried his name aloud.

'I am here, my love.' He was sitting beside her bed, but he rose at once and came to kiss her. Then he stroked her hair. 'You must rest,' he said tenderly. 'You were so brave, but you have had a terrible experience...'

'But you...?' She scanned his face with anxious eyes. 'Edward, you were hurt... I thought... Merton said that he had killed you.' She threw herself into his arms as the tears brimmed over.

'I am very much alive,' he teased. 'I hope to prove it to you when you are well again.'

'Don't joke!' She reached out a hand to touch his cheek. 'You were bleeding…'

'Just a superficial cut. Even the thickest head will bleed profusely; it looked worse than it was.'

'You make light of it, but, my dearest, you looked so dreadful…' She would not be convinced.

'Worse than usual?' The blue eyes twinkled as they looked into her own. 'I'll allow that I was a frightening sight.'

'Where did he strike you?' Gently she touched his head and found an alarming lump. He winced and drew her hand away. 'You should be in bed,' she announced.

'Nothing would please me more,' came the prompt reply. 'But had we not best wait until tonight? You are in no condition to welcome my advances.'

Georgiana's face grew rosy. 'You know I did not mean that you should make love to me,' she protested.

'I am ever hopeful…'

'Edward, be serious.'

'Very well.' He composed his face into an expression of polite interest. 'Madam, what is your will?'

'I want to know what happened. Merton…did he…did he escape the fire?'

He realised then that she had not seen the fearful sight which lived on in his mind, and he was glad of it. That blazing apparition was the stuff of nightmares.

He shook his head. 'He died in the blaze.'

'He was quite mad, you know.'

'I know. The ruin of his plans must have been the last straw.'

He was silent for some time, holding her as if he would never let her go.

'I should have listened to you, my dearest. You were never easy in your mind about him, were you?'

'You could not know that he would set the fire. Oh, Edward…all those people! If only we could have stopped him.' She buried her face against his coat.

'There was nothing we could do, Georgiana. His was an unhinged mind. Reason could not prevail, and he had all the cunning of a madman. I should have suspected treachery when he allowed me to take the torch.'

Georgiana began to shiver, but he soothed her into a calmer frame of mind.

'Betsy wishes to see you,' he said at last. 'Shall I ring for her?'

'Yes, please…and Scroggins too. My love, he tried to save me, but they held him back.'

'Did I not tell you that he was not quite the pillar of stiffness that you thought him?' Edward kissed her again. 'He has a high regard for you.'

Georgiana smiled doubtfully, but when Scroggins and Betsy entered the room she was forced to admit that he was right. The man looked deeply shaken and when he spoke it was with warmth.

'Madam, I am happy to see you safe,' he said. 'If there is anything your ladyship requires…anything I can do…?'

'You tried to do so much.' Georgiana gave him a radiant smile. 'You would have risked your life for me, I think.'

She was surprised to see him flush.

'Madam has been good to me and mine,' he replied. 'Betsy is but a country girl, and much patience is required…' He shot a sharp glance at his niece.

'Nonsense!' Georgiana beamed upon her maid. 'Betsy, you must not cry or you will soak the carpet.' She stretched out a hand and Betsy ran to her.

'Have I anything to wear?' she murmured. 'I still have my pearls…but apart from those…'

Edward rose from his seat beside her, and signalled to his man.

'It is time we left,' he said significantly. 'Madam will not be satisfied until she is allowed to leave her bed.' He looked at Georgiana with a grin. 'Betsy has a surprise for you, my love.' He was laughing as he left the room.

'What is it, Betsy?'

'Oh, miss…I mean madam…there's boxes of it. It was my uncle really… His lordship sent him out with orders… You'll never wear the half of it. Will I open the boxes for you?' In her eagerness the words came tumbling out.

At Georgiana's nod she began to unpack the gowns. Then her hands fell to her sides and she looked at her mistress with brimming eyes.

'What is it, Betsy?'

'Oh, madam, I thought you lost for sure…' She threw her apron over her head as she rocked to and fro in anguish.

'Now, Betsy, I won't have you "taking on" so.' Georgiana used the country expression deliberately, hoping to raise a smile. 'You must help me dress. His lordship tells me that Mr Harry is below…'

'He wanted to come up,' Betsy hiccuped between sobs. 'But the master said as he must wait.'

'Mr Harry is not a patient man,' Georgiana announced. 'If we don't hurry I shall face his wrath.'

'Oh, madam, I'm sorry.' Betsy looked crestfallen. Then she saw a twinkle in Georgiana's eyes, and she managed a reluctant smile. 'My lord would have something to say…'

She returned to her task, piling every surface high with gowns, underlinen, bonnets, ribbons, handkerchiefs and the prettiest of matching slippers.

'Where did it all come from?' Georgiana stared at the mounting heap in amazement. 'I had thought that gowns must be bespoke.'

'My uncle is what his lordship calls resourceful,' Betsy said proudly. 'He knows all the places…'

'I can well believe you. I wonder if the gowns will fit me?'

As she slipped into a pale blue muslin trimmed with matching ribbons she found that Scroggins had assessed both style and fit to perfection.

In wonder she stared at her reflection in the mirror. It didn't seem possible that the terrible events of the last few days had not changed her.

The great green eyes looked back at her. They had lost their haunted expression, but there was something there behind the smile. Sadness? No…not with Edward's love to warm her heart. Then she recognised it for what it was. She had grown up at last. It was a look of maturity.

A deep sense of joy possessed her, but she felt very calm as she made her way downstairs to join the others. Edward and Harry were waiting for her in a private room, and her brother hurried towards her as she entered. He caught her by the shoulders and looked into her eyes.

'Georgie, are you better? I've been out of my mind with worry.'

'I'm not even singed.' She smiled up at him.

'Sit down over here.' He guided her to a chair, still speaking in hushed tones. 'Is there anything I can get for you? Would you prefer to lie on the sofa? Should you be out of bed?' He was very pale and she realised that he was badly shocked.

'Don't be such a noddle-cock, Hal. I'm not at death's door.' The pithy words brought an injured look from Harry.

'You ain't lost your tongue, that's for sure.'

She twinkled at him. 'That's better! There's nothing like a quarrel to bring you to your senses…'

He tried to smile, but his face was grave.

'I have gone through hell in these past hours. It was all my fault, you know. If we had not met Merton this never would have happened.'

'Merton would have sought you out.' Edward regarded him calmly. 'He had reasons other than money to make use of you and Richard.'

'What do you mean?'

'The lady whom you thought I injured was his sister.'

Harry looked acutely uncomfortable. 'You should have told me…'

'I did not know myself until quite recently. And, Harry, I was not the villain you imagined. Georgie will tell you if you care to know.'

'No, no! I'll take your word for it. I expect that the gossips had only half the tale.'

'Thank you.' Edward returned his smile, and Harry's face began to clear.

'That, at least, is a relief,' he sighed. 'But when we heard about the fire…and that Merton had started it… Well, I tell you, neither Richard nor I would go through that again.'

'Don't think about it,' Georgiana pleaded. 'Merton is gone and we are safe.'

'He deserved to die. I won't say that I'm sorry. And it does make all the difference, doesn't it? Now we can return to England.'

Georgiana looked at him in astonishment.

'But…but I thought that you wished…that you had agreed to go to India?'

'I'd rather go back to London, wouldn't you? You must have missed it as I do. When I think of the balls, the parties…and all our friends…!'

Georgiana shot a despairing look at Edward, but he appeared to be absorbed in his newspaper.

Harry sensed her disquiet. 'I shan't be so foolish this time,' he promised. 'I'll choose my friends more carefully and there'll be no gambling. And, Georgie, you mustn't think that I shall always be on your doorstep. I'll visit you, of course, just once or twice a week, but I'll rent a house and—'

'Harry, listen to me. This will not do. You have given your word both to Edward and to me to take this opportunity with the East India Company.'

'But it may be years before I return. I shall not see you. Oh, Georgie, don't you want me…?'

She looked at his downcast head. 'I think you know how dear you are to me,' she replied gently. 'But life has changed for both of us. Did you not promise to make me proud of you? Why, you will come back with a fortune…'

He did not answer her, but she persevered.

'I believed you when you said that you had been through hell, my dear, but now you must look ahead. You are a man, with a man's responsibilities. In time you will take a wife and will have your own establishment…'

She stopped in dismay. She sounded as if she

was reading him a lecture. Edward came to the rescue.

'An interesting prospect,' he said drily. 'But Harry has not chosen his lady yet. Meantime, as a bachelor in India the world will be at his feet. There is racing, polo, excellent fishing in the north of the country, and the hunting is beyond compare. Imagine stalking a tiger...!'

Harry brightened, and his head went up.

'The social round is exhausting.' Edward continued in a bland tone. 'So many levees, dances and receptions... Harry may find them injurious to his health. Perhaps we should persuade him against the idea after all.'

'No, no! I have reconsidered. You may be right after all.' He stood up. 'Have you seen Richard?'

'He is out on some errand for me, but I believe you will find him on the Rue Saint Honore. You will dine with us tonight?'

Harry accepted gratefully and then he left them.

'Well done, my darling.' Edward smiled at his wife. 'I doubt if Harry will waver now.'

'Thanks to you. I sounded as if I was preaching at him, though I did not mean to do so.'

'You were a little circumspect, perhaps even

prim… I can't allow that.' Edward took her in his arms. 'You are much too beautiful to become a solemn matron.'

The slanting eyes gave him a mischievous look. 'You told me once that my appearance was deceptive,' she murmured. 'It is still so.'

'I can't be sure of that.' He held her at arm's length with a teasing look.

'I wonder how I can persuade you?'

'Minx! Would you flirt with your husband? Such improper behaviour calls for strong measures.' He kissed her until she was breathless.

'I could die against your lips,' she whispered.

'Far better to live, my darling, and live to the full. I may worship you with my body, but I love you with all my heart and soul.'

Glowing with happiness, she threw her arms about his neck. 'I wish I could tell you how I feel, but words are not enough.' She pressed a kiss into the hollow of his throat.

'In that we are agreed.' He gathered her close, laughing down at her. 'Perhaps there is another way…'

That night she gave herself to him without reservation. She had not thought it possible to love so fully. Then, with their passion spent, she nestled in the crook of his arm.

'Do you still think me prim, my lord?' she asked in a wicked whisper.

'Madam, you may keep your cool demeanour for the rest of the world. It won't deceive me again.' He bent his head and found her lips.

* * * * *

Invites *you* to experience lively, heartwarming all-American romances

Every month, we bring you four strong, sexy men, and four women who know what they want—and go all out to get it.

Enjoy stories about the pursuit of love, family and marriage in America today— *everywhere* people live and love!

AMERICAN *Romance*—
Heart, Home & Happiness

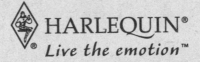

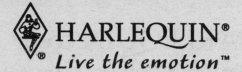

HARLEQUIN®
Live the emotion™

Upbeat,
All-American Romances

 flipside
Romantic Comedy

Harlequin Historicals®
Historical,
Romantic Adventure

HARLEQUIN®
INTRIGUE
Romantic Suspense

HARLEQUIN®
HARLEQUIN ROMANCE®
The essence of
modern romance

Seduction and passion
guaranteed

HARLEQUIN® *Super* ROMANCE®
Emotional,
Exciting, Unexpected

 *Temptation*

Sassy, Sexy, Seductive!

SILHOUETTE *Romance*®

Escape to a place where a kiss is still a kiss...

Feel the breathless connection...

Fall in love as though it were the very first time...

Experience the power of love!

Come to where favorite authors—such as

Diana Palmer, Stella Bagwell, Marie Ferrarella

and many more—deliver modern fairy tale romances and genuine emotion, time after time after time....

Silhouette Romance— from today to forever.

Silhouette®

Live the possibilities

V *Silhouette*®

SILHOUETTE *Romance*®

From first love to forever, these love stories
are fairy tale romances for today's woman.

Modern, passionate reads that are powerful and provocative.

Emotional, compelling stories that capture the intensity
of living, loving and creating a family in today's world.

V *Silhouette*®

I N T I M A T E   M O M E N T S™

A roller-coaster read that delivers romantic thrills
in a world of suspense, adventure and more.